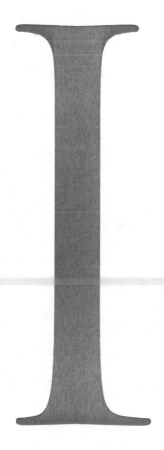

The Emolian Empire

Daniel Nelson III

TATE PUBLISHING
AND ENTERPRISES, LLC

Published by Tate Publishing & Enterprises, LLC
127 E. Trade Center Terrace | Mustang, Oklahoma 73064 USA
1.888.361.9473 | www.tatepublishing.com

Tate Publishing is committed to excellence in the publishing industry. The company reflects the philosophy established by the founders, based on Psalm 68:11,
"The Lord gave the word and great was the company of those who published it."

Book design copyright © 2015 by Tate Publishing, LLC. All rights reserved.
Cover design by Jeffrey Doblados
Interior design by Jomel Pepito

Published in the United States of America

ISBN: 978-1-63449-997-2
Fiction / Fantasy / Epic
14.11.13

Contents

Prologue

IMPRISONMENT

The deep chanting in the heart of Emolia called out to him. The melody was haunting but beautiful to his ears. He maneuvered towards it almost dancing at times. What a sound this melody was that interested him that no one wanted to be in the company of. As he drew near to the sound, he peeked over the high grass to the west to see a large gathering, which appeared to be in the middle of erecting something.

At once he noticed it was not just the elves building in their homeland, but all of the races had a hand in what looked to be a massive build in the flattest part of the hilly region. In the midst of the hypnotic chanting, he saw dwarves with precious metal that they toiled to craft using makeshift cauldrons and fire pits. He saw the graphite carry in hundreds of stones that had a hint of magic he could feel. Then he spied the humans that laid out paper that held the plans of the construct. Lastly, he peered upon the trolls and the orc who brought numbers and tools to piece it all together.

He watched them for days and nights. There were no breaks in the putting together of whatever it was he watched them do. A group would stop and another would take over. They appeared to dig a huge hole and then built around it. But what they constructed never reached into the sky. The chanting never stopped.

He had never seen them work together at anything they had done this intently. It bothered him to not know what the assembly was building but their chanting, oh so amused him. After a particular groups portion of the construct was done, they would leave and not return. He kept mind on all of them. After three weeks of building, only a select few remained. Two from each race stood with hoods on and continued the ongoing chant around the finished project.

He then approached the site. Before he reached the structure, he noticed hundreds of unlit torches that surrounded the structure. Every one of the torches was resting in a gold stand and dripped a repulsive solution. Without a thought, he walked into the site still enjoying the chants. The ones who stood around the construct and chanting bothered him not. Silently he passed them and touched the huge stone sides that had words written on them that he could not read. Curious, he walked the entire rectangular perimeter around the stone sides to discover it was massive.

Then he climbed to the top of the stone sides to see another slab that was on top of the first. It was not as tall and sat in the center of the base. Effortlessly he lifted inches off of the structure and floated over more words he could not read on the second slab. This stone had huge hinges on it that connected it to the base. Now humming the chant himself, he walked around to see that it had a split in the middle and hinges on the other side. A door, he thought.

His need to know what lay behind the huge door got the best of him. Intrigued, he walked back to the split and folded his arms to put his hands on his chest. Then he opened his arms and the two huge stones opened as if to swallow the sky. The noise from them opening was deafening, but the chant could still be heard. *What could be below?* he wondered, *Could it be gold, jewels, a powerful weapon, or even an entrance to a secrete hall?* He walked up to the edge of the opening to see only darkness.

"Why would anyone construct something so massive around a huge hole?" he asked himself.

He then conjured fire in his hand and dropped it in to the pit to get a glimpse of what may be inside. The flame just fell into darkness. The races standing around the structure then stopped the chant, he ran to the edge to see them. As he reached the edge and looked down, the flame he dropped consumed the pit and rushed back up tenfold and spewed into the sky, lighting it up. The flame fell back from the sky onto the torches lighting them all. This he did not like.

"You there," he called out to one of the hooded figures who stood on the perimeter. "What is this place?"

The figure did not answer him.

"Insect, do you know who I am? I would advise you to tell me what this place is?" His voice became aggravated and began to sound monstrous.

They all spoke back to him at the same time and began to move towards the outer rim of the site.

"I know who you are. That is why I summoned you here with the song your father sang to you in the heavens." said the being who was questioned.

"Who are you?" he asked.

"I am the future that you cannot touch." he said.

The ten then walked past the torches.

"I will touch you all and paint this structure with your blood." He said as he rushed from the top of the structure out to the torches.

In a blink of an eye, he was upon the perimeter and reached out to grab two of the ten but could not pass the lit torches.

"I see what this is now. A futile trap, how long do you think it will hold me?" he asked the two in front of him as he moved to the next two. "How long?" he asked as he moved to the next two, then the next. "How long will this hold me? Not long at all, it feels as if this will only hold until the morning, then I will hunt you all down and kill you."

He then reached the last two. An elfin woman in a grey cloak and a being in a black cloak he could not make out. The being in the black cloak spoke.

"This will not hold you long. Upon the sun's rise the spell will be broken, but we will be nowhere that you can find us, and when the sun rises you will be greeted by your prison. The next time we are this close will be before this after now."

The ten beings began to fade away, the one in the black cloak being the last. Before he faded away, he removed his hood and the one that could not cross the torches saw his face.

"You." the being said in disgust. "I will see you again elf and take your life when I do!"

He went back to the structure and noticed that all the words he could not read were illuminated by his own power. Looking to the sky he noticed the torches' power reached to the heavens. Powerless to move beyond the torches, he perched himself on the edge of the structure and waited for the suns to rise.

The sun rose from the east and the flames that lit the torches dissipated. At once he rose from his perch and lifted into the air in an attempt to leave the structure and find its creators. As he reached the very point on the other side of the torches, a loud whistle then crackling sound moved through the air, and he was met by a fireball the size of a comet that struck him and sent him crashing back into the plot around the structure. The dust settled from the impact, and he moved swiftly to the top of the structure. Intently he looked to the sky and saw them darken with dragons he counted and felt for them, 364 was his estimation. The day had come that he must answer for his transgressions against Xahmore` but he would make sure his aggressors pay dearly for their participation. Viciously he let out an intimidating roar as he transformed himself into a hideous winged monster, inviting them all to death.

"Come, come and find your deaths in your attempt upon me. Pray to your creator as I pull the life from your bodies and devour your existence. There is no avoiding my wrath neither now nor in the days ahead. Even if you succeed in putting me behind this door, I will one day be freed and come to slaughter the rest of you. Let it begin!" said the great beast of Xahmore.

1

Tell Us of Him

Here they come, humph, just as they always do when the clans gather. The young elves named, Lorameck and Feloshia have come to Glimack hill on the far side of the Genesis Valley that looks upon the dead mountain Maysor. My seventh generation of offspring has come once again to see me, but not for hugs and laughs they've come for stories of the heroes that have long ago been forgotten and battles that are only now folklore among the drunks in taverns across all of Xahmore`. They've come for a glimpse into the past that will light up their young eyes and fill their spirits with adventure. For there are things that grow old, this scene is one that remains forever young to me.

"Greetings, Wise Elder!" says the young elfin boy.

"Salutations, young Lorameck, you look as if you will be wielding a bow and arrow soon." I say with a hint of peaked interest.

He sticks his chest out and his voice gets deeper.

"Yes, Wise Elder, I shall. I am scheduled for weapons training upon the arrival of the new moon."

"Good, good, we will need more warriors like you in the days to come. Who is this fair lady you have with you today?" I say as I lean over and touch her nose slightly with my index finger.

"Greetings, Wise Elder!" she says with a slight giggle.

"Ah, greetings, little Feloshia, you look as beautiful as the Elfin Queen Emona herself." I lean forward in my seat to bow with one hand to the side.

She smiles and sways back and forth showing her joy in my comment.

"How is your mother, Lorameck?" I ask.

"She is fine. She prepares with the other women for the feast that will take place in the valley before the great rains." He replies as a male would.

"Wonderful! What news of your father, any word of him?" I ask.

"The last we heard, he was still holding his position in the flat lands against the Ogres of Lundo." He replies as a soldier would.

"Yes, yes, Lundo, the Ogres there are very powerful, but Welohiem is a great warrior, the Ogres will not move him." I comment as interested as he wanted me to be.

"Wise Elder, you sit here before the sun rises and after it has gone again with your chest to that dead mountain and that hood over your head. How long will you sit here?" he asks as a child would.

"I will sit here until Xahmore` shakes below us all young Lorameck." I reply then change the subject to why they really have come to see me. "So young ones, what makes you come to see this old elf?" I ask leaning upon my large cane.

"Feloshia and I would love to hear tales of the past, Wise Elder. Please tell us one." Lorameck says.

"Perhaps some other time, there is much work to do before the feast." I kidded loudly.

"Please, Wise Elder, we have completed our chores for the great feast. Please!" they both wined.

"Ahhh very well, what shall it be? The human lord Trevaughn's voyages in the deep wood of Amblar, or the tiny winged hero Evermore's journey to the Lava Sea, maybe the beast master Darius who thwarted the Qualin invasion with thousands of rats as his army, perhaps the thieves of the smoke guild's adventure to steal the bracelets of the snow beast Grok, or would you like to hear of how Dark Soul the elf freed the province of Drugshaw from the dragon Al'Draze, the battle was glorious!" I stated as I flailed my arms about to make the stories seem larger than life.

They looked at me unamused.

"All of those stories sound great, Wise Elder, but Feloshia and I would like to hear about I. He was supposed to be the most powerful of all elves, as legend tells it. The warrior elves say he was faster than any animal, stronger than a great troll, and skilled in all arts of fighting and weaponry! Do you know stories of him?" Lorameck asked like an eager student.

I had to sit back in my chair and dwell for a moment; I hadn't heard that name in many years past.

"Yes, young ones, I know many stories of the blotted elf known as I. He did posses great power, great power indeed, but it was also at times considered a curse upon him." I said.

"A curse, Wise Elder?" asked Feloshia.

"Yes, little Feloshia, a curse. You see the world now has many blotted elves, take us for instance, our skin is all black, but look into your brother's eyes are they not the color of any other thousand eyes you have ever seen, and when you smile do not your teeth show white as the snow atop lost giant's mountain?"

Many, many hundreds of years ago there were very few blotted elves; no one knows how they came to be. Dark magic some say, others say it was an experiment by Ulgrah "the Mad," and even that a black dragon took elfin form because he fell in love with a beautiful elf named Elaughier, but the story says when they first appeared the telling of the coming of the black eyed elf was true and but a matter of time.

Oh some of the most powerful beings in Xahmore` waged war on the elves because they thought the black-eyed blotted elf would be too powerful and would overthrow them when he arrived. But the elves would not give their blotted brothers away to any nation of troll, orc, human, dwarf, or graphite. All of them knew of the story that was told before writing, that there would be an elf with blotted skin and eyes that would be twin to the color of the Onyx of Crimlo, his mouth would be as dark as the dwarves from the coal mines of Eastgrip, that he would be as a shadow in his brightest days and would one day save us all from the name that would wake all evil.

The blotted elves were protected and moved around Xahmore` for centuries! Many being slaughtered, some captured by other nations and made to breed hoping the black-eyed blotted elf would be born under their watch, so they could control his power. Then the foretold day on the Pixie island of Omagasa, an elf only eighty-eight years of age named Dinora gave birth to the black-eyed baby Xahmore` had so long waited for.

The slayer of the beast was with us." I said to their amazement.

2

Dark Blessing

The moment he was born, the sun was the hottest it had ever been. When it reached its highest point in the sky, both of our moons in their opposite rotations aligned to eclipse it. The world was pitch black, all forms of light vanished. Then as all of Xahmore` cried out in fear and anguish, the child's first breath and exhale into a cry coincided with creators will for the moons to move and all light to come back to Xahmore`.

Word of his birth alone ended the slaughter and the taking of the blotted elf. All wars waged on elfin kind stopped, and nations began to fear the clergy of King Telaris Emolian, for the mightiest warrior had been born to the elves. It was a truly glorious day; legend says that all of Xahmore's righteous celebrated and the wicked plotted for the baby's death.

I was born smaller than the average elf and appeared he may die within his first week of life. His heartbeat and breathing would stop at every new moon in his first year. Blenadrene, an elfin wizard, told Dinora not to fret, that it was because of a connection with the spirit side of the universe that the child had. He told her that elders of long ago would come and tell him the stories of the times before.

"The spirit world? Why would spirits come to him and take him to their plane of existence?" asked Lorameck.

"Because, young Lorameck, I was here to save more than the living plane but existence itself. Not many alive knew this."

As he began to grow, he was many years ahead of his age, he walked within his first three months of life, he ran as fast as the prairie cats of Jysham before he was seven, and was able to overpower elves a hundred years his senior when he had only been living thirteen years.

He was small in stature and light in weight for most of his early years. His hair was locked but not long enough to cover his long curved ears.

He was taught many different fighting styles from masters that would visit the island for one reason or another, learning in days what took most years. All of his muscles were well defined within his slim frame, and his intelligence rivaled that of the most scholarly of elves. But he was still a child.

He enjoyed occasional mischief and frolicking with friends he had made on the island. Once he and Mlar, his best friend who was a pixie, journeyed onto a beach of the island that had been forbidden to all and were attacked by a blothar, a fierce bear-like creature that towered above I four times over. The beast growled as he circled the two friends with his eyes set on the meal in front of him. I told his friend to fly from harm's way and to tell his mother what had become of him.

As Mlar rose quickly from the ground, the blothar charged. I stood as a warrior eight hundred years his senior. The monster's steps pounded the ground and his growls vibrated the air. With his last few steps, the blothar stood and began to swipe down at I with his deadly paw and with one swift touch to the throat of the beast, I moved to the side and watched the beast fall dead. Mlar flew back to his friend in awe.

"How did you slay that beast with such ease?" Mlar asked still afraid.

"At the final moment before the creature struck down, I was able to see a black hole in its throat and reached out and touched it. I did not know the creature would fall dead, but just followed what I felt." I replied calmly.

"Wow!" Mlar said with wide eyes and a goofy smile.

This ability to see the spirit plane got stronger as I got older and at times allowed him to see plainly the living world and the spiritual realm side by side. Ghosts walking among the living, demonic spirits hovering over the most-wicked of men and those who were confused, angelic spirits watching over families and protecting children from harm. Oh this child was special very special indeed.

3

WISDOM OF THE UNKNOWN

The one being that had more influence over I than any other was his mother. He adored her so. He always brought her flowers or little gifts to make her smile. Once he even carved a wooden statue of them holding hands. He was very protective of her and would fight at a moments notice, if he felt she was disrespected in anyway.

I's mother Dinora was a beautiful elfin sorceress, her blotted skin was smooth, her eyes were a misty grey; she was tall for a female elf and described by her teacher Blenadrene as a quick study. Her parents where slain when they attempted to escape a graphite horde that found one of the protected blotted elf villages. She managed to escape because her father sacrificed himself to hold off the pursuing members of the horde. After days of running, she came upon the fishing docks of Dwaleel. She stowed her way upon a fishing ship headed to the tiny pixie island and was discovered by a wizard, Blenadrene. He was hundreds of years older than her and acted as her father. She studied magic under Blenadrene, the most humble but most powerful of the Wizards of the Yorenzana. Blenadrene was a tall, handsome, smooth-faced, and muscular elf with a maple-colored skin, green eyes, and always wore a brown tattered wool cloak.

Both were on the boat to the Pixie Island to hide for different reasons. I believe it was fate they found one another; any other wizard may have been tempted to control the powerful child when it was born. Blenadrene watched after the two as if they were his own daughter and grandson.

He once left in secrecy to destroy an armada of humans that approached the island. They somehow learned of the child's location and had come to take him. It was not even a fight, Blenadrene caused the water to swallow the ships and feed the murky depths of the sea. Before he returned, he cast a spell that could just be seen from the coast of the island. The spell circled the island in a thick fog that read the heart and mind so anyone who came for the child with evil intent would be lost in it forever. This fog was called the ring of Omegasa by all who traveled the sea. Being so young and in love with her son, Dinora cried for her baby boy often. She knew her son's destiny and that his journey would be difficult. She named him I, not because of the deep black eyes that he had as most thought, but because she knew one day he must stand alone and save us.

In writings and the stories handed down about I, his father was unknown. Some say Dinora was impregnated by a being of awesome power that was not an elf at all; other rumors say she was lifted to the heavens and given the seed. The Recorders say that Dinora was courted by an ancient elf no one had seen for countless centuries or since the conception of I. But all of the particulars are nothing compared to the fact that he had come!

Dinora studied and practiced her craft ruthlessly so that she could be as powerful as she could to protect her son.

Blenadrene taught her technique upon technique, spell upon spell, and secret after secret.

During a session, I once peaked in to hear the student and the teacher dispute about a spell that Blenadrene would never teach Dinora.

"Then why teach me at all?" yelled Dinora.

"I do this for you because I know you will protect the boy with your life, and if you are to lose it protecting him, you will not do so weakly!" Blenadrene proclaimed.

She responded, "I understand master, so why won't you teach me the spell of Leana."

"A spell of that magnitude will destroy you, so I will not! You will have to make do without it." He said authoritatively.

She would ask him again and again and he would deny her.

4

THE FIVE ELDERS

When I was about twenty years old, that fateful morning came. The sunrise that changed I's life forever. The sun came over the horizon and eased over the land of Omegasa pushing the darkness back like a spirit caught in a light wind. The light peaked over the windowsill in I's room and touched his face. He woke up and the sun continued to fill his room with light, and as it filled, he realized he was in the company of five beings. There was an old elf, a very muscular dwarf, a beautiful human woman, a massive troll that had to take a knee and still struggled to fit in the room, and a blind orc who stood on the other side of the room. He greeted them as any child should greet any noble, and they were in shock.

The eldest of the visitors asked the young elf, "How is it you see us, child?"

I replied, "Do you not exist, and are you not standing here before me?"

The old elf smiled shook his head looked to the other nobles and said, "Then the Withering is now upon us."

I was told it was time for him to leave the island and that he should travel with the old elf and the other nobles to the Emolian Empire where he would have refuge from the days of the beast.

"Why should I hide?" asked I.

"Because when you are older, wiser, and stronger you will be the one to save all existence from the beast that will change the shape of Xahmore` for the living and the dead." said the old elf.

"My mother and Blenadrene will protect me until I am able to protect you all." scarfed I more so at the thought of hiding than the old elf.

"Young elf, the powers of your mother and Blenadrene combined cannot protect you from what is to come, we are the ones sent who will protect you and prepare you to learn what you need in order to protect us all. If you do not believe me, tell Blenadrene you spoke to Lomerian Centurial, and you will know you must leave with us as soon as possible in order to survive!" the old elf stated.

I sprinted from his chambers causing a gust of wind. He found Blenadrene who was in meditation and told him of the five nobles who appeared in his room. He told him of how he was told of the days of the beast, and how he should travel to the empire with the nobles in order to survive. In all of I's frantic talk Blenadrene kept his meditation intact floating a few feet above ground. I then told him that the elfin noble who spoke these things to him was Lomerian Centurial, and Blenadrene opened his eyes wide, took a knee, and bowed his head.

"Blenadrene, what do say of these words?" asked I.

"Young one who is to save us all, you will do as Lomerian Centurial has instructed."

"Who is he? He said you knew of him." said the young blotted elf.

"He was the most powerful wizard of his time and my master! He told me before he died that his mission would be greater in the after than here on Xahmore`. He is now here to guide you were no one else can, we must prepare for the days ahead and you must follow him." Blenadrene replied.

I returned to his chambers at what seemed to be a snail's pace. With his head hung low and his feet dragging he walked through the village, he reached the doorway and the nobles all looked at him with the most serious of stares.

"What have you learned, young protector?" asked Lomerian.

"I will leave with you but I must warn my people of the days that lie ahead." said I.

"I would expect no less of you, do what you must. We will return when it is time to leave." said Lomerian.

5

INTO THE FOG

I went to the center of the village of Quiller where the colony of the island would meet every morning for a meal. He proceeded to warn them of the days to come. He told them of the journey he must take into the Emolian Empire and urged them all to do the same. Some agreed, some decided to stay. Over the next week, ships were prepared, food was gathered, and families uprooted for the three month voyage.

On the day that the boats were to leave, the nobles appeared to I once again and told him he was not to accompany the boats east, but he would make the journey with them.

"Why must I leave my people?" Asked I.

"There are things you must experience and trials you must face before you reach the Emolian Empire. No one else would be able to follow. When you leave this island, all of Xahmore` will be concerned of your whereabouts and that would be deadly to anyone around you." said Lomerian.

I agreed. He said farewell to his mother who griped him with all of her might.

"Be brave and return to me." She said with tears in her beautiful grey eyes.

"I promise I will, mother." said I.

"Be humble and learn all Lomerian has to teach you I." said Blenadrene with a proud look upon his face.

"I will." The young elf replied.

He bid his friends safe travel and said he would see them when he reached the empire. He watched the boats pull away from the docks with his mother crying until they one by one disappeared into the fog. He stood looking out at the fog for a long while. A tear dropped from his eye to his cheek then onto the beach sand.

"Young elf," spoke the oldest noble. "Your journey to destiny begins now! Bring nothing with you and discover how all the world will unite around you!"

I dropped everything he had and was left with only the cloth that covered his mid section. Lomerian levitated I and took him out over the water to the edge of the fog.

"Look, young one, look at how evil will come against you!!"

I looked out into the water and the noble elf waved his hand to dispel the fog and revealed to I thousands upon thousands of ships that had come in search of him and become lost in Blenadrene's spell. I stared in amazement!

"Do you see how important you are, young elf? Countless hordes of evil have come to seek you out to kill, enslave, or turn you to their ways, and countless more will try," Lomerian proclaimed.

The master wizard waved his arms and reset the fog. I was then dropped into the water and began to swim towards the fog. When he reached the edge of it, he could feel the powerful magic it possessed. When he was in the thick of the fog, he saw the five elders watching him in the distance. When he reached the outer edge of the fog he was greeted by the blind Orc.

6

THE CALM

"What has happened to the other nobles?" asked I.

"They will return at the appointed time, young elf. Now you will begin your training." The Orc said in a subtle voice as he dropped a wooden staff into the water. "Catch the staff and stand upon it."

The staff began to move through the water at a great speed causing the water to be uneasy, and off I went behind it swimming fiercely. A storm brewed like witchcraft in seconds from nowhere. The water became so uneasy that waves seemed to raise high enough to graze the sky. The staff stayed just out of arms reach as I swam behind it for what seemed like hours until the staff darted off into the horizon at a speed that split the water and caused it to crash down on I. Lightning crackled causing the sky and sea to be seen as plain as day, and thunder rolled making it the only thing able to be heard.

When he finally made it back to the top side, the blind Orc walked upon the water over to him and asked, "How does a lifeless object move so fast that you cannot catch it?"

"I do not know, noble Orc." I treaded the waters and thought until the staff returned to rise up from the water and smack him in the face.

After regaining his composure, I noticed the staff floating nearby and eased over to it, only to see it dart away from him again making the water more uneasy, and again he gave chase to the staff for what this time took days. The storm raged on and became more belligerent. Time and time again the staff would speed away and send waves crashing back on I.

"Days will pass, kingdoms will crumble, the most powerful beings will return to the essence. In it all there is but one thing that lives before, during, and after what has been created, what is that, young elf?" asked the Orc.

"It is hard for me to think under these conditions, Orc, I do not know." I said in a frustrated tone.

"You are not far from the answer, young elf. What holds a philosopher's tongue, wins a woman's heart, and makes a general greater than the sword?" asked the Orc.

"I do not know, wise Orc." said I.

"To solve this riddle is to be delivered from your dilemma." stated the Orc.

And again and again the blind Orc would ask the question, "How does a lifeless object move so fast that you cannot catch it?"

I thought hard as he treaded the water. He was now exhausted and at his wits end when the staff returned and smacked him this time he paid it no mind and the staff laid still upon the water. He floated there peacefully upon his back and no movement was made by the staff or the water. The storm let up slowly. I laid upon his back long enough to watch the sun rise and set twice. The staff laid still and the water remained calm. The storm subsided into a faint drizzle.

I looked towards the Orc, smiled then swam toward the staff, and again the staff darted off at the blinding speed that caused the waves to crash on I, but the water did not become uneasy, and I was only a hands grasp away from the staff swimming at an unheard of pace. Then he took two powerful strokes and hurled himself from the water to land atop the staff and glide across the water. The water remained calm and after nineteen days the chase had come to an end, and I stood upon the staff.

"The answer to your riddle is thought, wise Orc. A thought created, lived with creation, and will live on after creation. Thought is what holds a philosopher's tongue, wins a woman's heart, and makes a general greater than the sword." I stated with a smile.

The Orc then asked the question again, "How does a lifeless object move so fast that you cannot catch it?"

And I answered, "The object only moved because I believed that it would, and it moved so fast that I could not catch it because I believed I could not catch it. When I took doubt from my mind, the staff moved because I wanted it to and then I knew that I could move as fast as I could think." Then I stepped from the staff onto the water towards his teacher then said, "When the mind is clear, anything is possible." I looked to the sky and then took a knee to show respect for the lesson he had learned and for the trial that taught him the lesson.

The blind Orc told I, "Keep the staff, young one, so that it may remind you of the peace you have found this day and the goal that was set for you and reached. For we are in your mind, and the water is now calm and able to be navigated upon."

"What is your name, wise Orc, that I may know who has helped me calm the seas of my mind?" asked the young thankful elf.

"I have no name, I am not on the same side of the spiritual plane as the others, I have not yet passed into the realms of the living, so I have not been given a name." The Orc then faded into the atmosphere.

7

THE DWARF AND THE TROLL

The ring of mist crept across the face of the water like a tired ghost and a large hand came across I's shoulder from behind. Before I could react, he was pushed down into the water to his lower jaw bone. He tried to fight the hand off, but he could not move. The water had become solid.

The ring eased away slowly and a few feet in front of him, I saw two massive figures— the troll and dwarf. The troll towered over the dwarf in height but the muscular build of the dwarf made them both awesome.

As the mist went completely away, I found himself buried in hot beach sand. The two imposing figures laughed and told the elf to free himself.

"I cannot move, how am I supposed to free myself from such a trap?" he asked while he struggled to move.

"Can you not move at all, young protector?" said the troll mockingly.

"No, I cannot!" he yelled in response.

"Then how do you plan on protecting Xahmore?" snarled the troll. "I should bite your head off and save our time here in eternity..."

"Enough, Blygor!" commanded the dwarf. "Young elf, I was in a similar situation in Maygar, left for dead by my treacherous guild, and I made it out to slaughter them all as you will make it out and save us all!"

"But I can only move the smallest and weakest parts of my body!" whined the elf.

"Well then, young one, I would suggest you start there!" the dwarf said impatiently.

He then walked back to where the troll was and took a seat and stared at the young elf.

I began to twiddle his pinky fingers and matching toes. After a few minutes the muscles controlling these digits became exhausted and he could move them no more. A discouraged look came over his face.

"With every struggle, your being becomes stronger." grumbled the dwarf.

I rested until the pain left his muscles and began to move his fingers and toes again. After a few hours, the sand had shifted so that one by one he could move each finger and toe. He was exhausted and began to fall asleep. He looked up to see the dwarf staring at him and the troll snapping a tree on the beach in half. He could no longer stay awake and fell asleep.

When I awoke he was in complete darkness. *Am I dead,* he thought, *is this another test?* He tried to move and realized he was still stuck in the sand. He screamed a frustrated cry. In the middle of his howl, he heard loud steps coming towards him, and suddenly there was the light of the sun that blinded him momentarily. When he regained his vision, he saw the troll walking back to the dwarf with a large dome structure he leaned up against, the other half of the tree he had made it from.

"Did you sleep well, young one?" asked the dwarf.

"Yes, I did, as well as can be expected being completely submerged in dirt!" he said sarcastically.

"Good, now that you have wasted a whole day resting, why don't you spend as long getting yourself free!" yelled the troll.

"Why did you cover my head while I slept?" asked the blotted elf.

"Because I did not want to see anything else bite your head off before I get the chance!" growled the troll.

"Surely you will, troll, surely you will." said I smirking.

I began to move his hands and feet swirling all of the sand he could touch, loosening up what seemed to be a granule here and there until….the sand sunk to the middle of his neck. Then he rested looking up at the dwarf who just stared at him.

"He will try and rip you're head off first, your neck does not look strong enough to stop him." laughed the dwarf.

I noticed that the sand moving that much had loosened around his body, enough for him to barely move, but enough to move nonetheless. He began shifting and moving every part of his body in such a way that every muscle was used until exhaustion set in yet again. I looked up at the dwarf again to see him staring at him without emotion as he had been doing. Right before I passed out, he heard the loud steps again and the dome was replaced by the troll as he slipped into sleep.

8

PRECIOUS TEARS

The night sky had few clouds so the moonlight was allowed to gaze upon the great sea. Dinora stood at the bow of the lead ship in a meager fleet of four, worried about her young son. There was an old dwarf who came on deck with a small wooden instrument that had strings made from grand cat whiskers.

"Ah I see that I am not alone this fair night." said the small dwarf. "Would my lady have a request that she would like me to play?" He showed his small instrument and smiled at Dinora while making his eyebrows move up and down.

She smiled back slightly to be courteous. "Do you know the song of Shylah Clomaur?"

"Indeed I do, but why such a sad song on this beautiful night?" asked the dwarf who became concerned.

"I need to hear something that matches the pain in my heart, so I will not seem so alone." she replied.

The dwarf nodded and walked over to a place he could sit comfortably and began to play the song. He pulled the strings with such emotion that the sounds touched the soul of all the ears it graced.

Light winds caused Dinora's hair to lift and wave in the wind as smooth as the water the ships drifted upon. She had never been apart from I for more than a few hours, and now they would be apart for months. The times she cared for him flashed through her mind. The times she held him, put potion on scrapes and cuts, prepared his meals, and watched him play.

The dwarf's playing of the Shylah Clomaur became more graceful. Tears began to flow from her eyes and trickle down her beautiful face. The first droplet that left her face turned into a diamond and landed on the banister which she was leaning.

She was startled.

"Your tears are too precious to let escape from your beautiful eyes, Dinora." said Blenadrene. "What troubles you?"

"I am worried about my son, master, he is but a baby and is out there alone. What if something terrible happens to him?" she asked.

"He is not alone, my old master guides him, and I is foretold to have great power. He should be able to take care of himself if he has to." Blenadrene said in an attempt to comfort the worried mother.

"That is easy to say, but he is my son, it is a mother's duty to have concern for her child no matter how destined they are for greatness." she expressed.

The dwarf reached the break in the song that was to last a few seconds and the silence was only interrupted by the waves that washed up against the boats, and the breeze that meshed with the song of the seas.

Blenadrene just looked at Dinora and began to empathize with her.

The dwarf began to play again, this time with a passion that spilled from his heart to the strings.

"I miss him also, Dinora. I was there for his birth, first steps, and first words. I watched him master arts, skills, and simple tricks in his short time here. I feel for him as my own. But the time has come for him to be our protector and even though we may have concern for his survival and well being, our separation from him is necessary, we will not be able to help him do all things. Some he will have to do alone." The wizard explained.

The dwarf finished the song and just sat there looking out into the sea as if he had also steered up some emotion in himself with the song.

"I know, master, but I can only imagine what he is going through without us to protect him." Dinora whined.

Blenadrene took the diamond from the banister walked over to the dwarf and handed it to him.

"Would you mind playing that once more, Lindle?" Blenadrene asked calmly.

"Not at all, Blenadrene, not at all." the dwarf replied with the utmost respect.

As he walked back to Dinora, the dwarf began the song again. The two embraced, and Dinora cried as the ships continued on their way towards Emolia with the song intimately blending with the air.

9

ANSWER

I was awoken by the most awful smell he had ever inhaled. His black eyes opened to the troll's face directly in front of his, breathing and grunting heavily. The troll's breathe smelled like rotten meat and hot melons, and his body smelled like an overworked field beast.

"What is taking you so long, young elf? I have all of eternity to wait, so there is no need to stall!" barked the troll.

"I am not stalling, great troll, I am inside of my destiny and time has appointed a meeting for us. You will wish fate had stalled when that appointed time comes." responded I.

The troll was infuriated and roared in I's face. Saliva dripped from the two large tusks in his lower jaw. His eyes filled with blood that showed his rage from the young elf's comment. He stood then reached down with his massive hand and palmed I's head in an attempt to crush it. I screamed out in pain.

As he began to squeeze, the dwarf stood and spoke commanding words to the troll.

"Release his head and wait as has been told!"

The troll snarled at the dwarf released his grip and stomped back to where he would wait.

I began to move his body and realized he had more freedom to move and began to swirl his arms and legs in every motion possible until it felt as if though he were swimming in the sand.

The dwarf's stare changed from one of no emotion to a look of discovery. He looked over at the troll and smirked and looked back at the young elf moving in the sand.

I's body again began to tire. So for the next twenty-one raisings of the dome from I's head and the continuous moving in the sand, the tirade continued between the elf and troll.

The dwarf watched and everyday his cold stare got warmer until he seemed to be amused by what was taking place.

On the twenty-fourth raising of the dome, the troll yelled out in anger.

The dwarf rose from his spot to see that the head of the blotted elf was no longer in the sand.

"Where is he?" shouted the troll as he sifted through the sand with his free hand.

The dwarf began to laugh much to the dislike of the troll.

"Rune, why do you laugh? When I find the elf I will break him in two, and you laugh?" said the angered troll.

"You have the elf right where you have wanted him all along, Blygor, now what will you do with him?" Rune said laughing.

The troll stood to his feet with a confused look on his face and yelled to the dwarf, "I wanted him in my hands and he is no longer here!" The troll threw his arms into the air and roared.

The dwarf began to laugh uncontrollably, pointing at the troll as he became more and more frustrated.

The massive troll then turned over the dome he had constructed out of tree and vine and was greeted by a blow from the young elf's fist. *Whamm!*

The blow struck the massive troll so hard, it snapped the sharp top off of his left tusk and sent the troll to the ground with a large thump. He dropped the dome and before it hit the ground, I parted with it and landed feet first in a crouching position on the beach.

The troll shook off the powerful blow and turned to see the young elf who had struck him.

I's body had undergone a miraculous transformation. Still slender but all of his muscles had increased twice in size, were as hard as stone, and as defined as a master recorder's lessons.

The troll snarled and charged I.

I was amazed at what the time's toil in the sand had done to his body, and in marveling at his own physique, he looked up just in time to see the troll's shoulder lower and braced himself for the impact.

Thwoooom!

The sound from the impact sent birds flying from the trees and I flying through them. He hit and snapped three Gattalahen trees before he was lodged into the fourth. He looked up to see the troll charging yet again. He shifted his body and snapped the thick tree in two. Catching the top half and slinging it at the troll who smacked it into pieces.

Blygor looked to locate the elf, only to feel a painful kick landing to the top of his head. The troll shrieked out in pain and landed upon a knee. I ran at him to attack and was smacked to the ground.

I stood and the fight continued. They traded the fiercest blows each could muster. After each was bloody and breathing hard, I leapt into the thick bush that surrounded the area.

"You may be strong, elf, but your strength is no match for mine, and your trickery and speed will only evade me for so long!" Blygor yelled out.

"I am not evading you, foolish beast, I am merely waiting for our destinies to collide and leave you at my mercy!" I's voice seemed to say from every side of the wood.

The troll tore the brush apart looking for his adversary, pulling up bushes, knocking over trees, until he felt a pain in the back of his neck from an elbow delivered from the young elf. This blow brought him to both his knees.

The young elf walked around to the front side of the Troll to deliver another awesome blow. He leaped up to strike and the troll caught his punch in his mighty palm. The troll then smiled at I, with his broken tusk and rotten teeth, and struck I with a blow that knocked I back to the beach.

"You are doing better than I expected, young elf!" laughed the dwarf from his cozy spot.

I stood to his feet and saw the Troll charging yet again this time with fury in his eyes.

"Why do you run to your destiny when it has no warm embrace for you?" asked I tauntingly.

The great troll was overcome with anger and charged even harder at I. I watched as the troll became enraged and charged almost uncontrollably. Every step the troll took towards I shook the beach. I stood his ground gazing at the troll's rapid approach with no fear. The dwarf stood as if to recognize the end of the battle drew near. The troll let out a hideous battle cry as he was just a few more steps from the blotted elf and lowered his head to try and impale I with his massive horns. The young elf crouched low with is legs spread to strengthen his stance. The troll's battle cry became more furious as he closed in for the kill.

As the troll reached the blotted elf, I, with the quickness and elusiveness of a sea serpent, grabbed the troll's hair with his left hand and the jaw with his right. Using the troll's momentum and his newly gained strength I flung the troll from the beach into the deep murky waters of the Multrag Sea. The troll, who could not swim, began to splash around for his life but to no avail as he sunk below the water's surface.

I fell to his back in pain and exhaustion.

The dwarf walked over to the young elf and looked at him with a smile, picked him up and said, "Well done, young one, well done."

Rune draped the elf across his shoulder and walked into the dark jungle.

"Strength is nothing without courage, and you have proven you possess both on this day." The dwarf reaffirmed to I.

The dwarf carried I into the heart of the jungle where there was a fire that lit the dark woods.

I looked up to see what appeared to be a thief's camp with all types of weapons lined up around it.

"Make us proud, young warrior." said Rune, as he disappeared.

10

HIDDEN TREASURE

The lower deck of the lead ship creaked as he walked silently towards her quarters. Sweat was on his brow as he staggered through the dimly-lit hall. The rocking of the ship from the heavy waves did not help his cause. He turned right and could see her door at the end of the hall. The slight tilting of the ship made his footing seem as if he stood on oil. He fell to his knees and saw a pixie talking to a huge snake.

"Is that you, Blenadrene? Are you alright?" Mlar asked.

"Mlar, I am fine just a little bothered by the sea's movement. Are you actually talking to a snake or am I delusional?" he asked the pixie.

"I know it is odd but I seem to understand her, I met her about a month ago in the back of the galley." Mlar said as he rubbed his hand across the snake's head.

"A pixie beast master? Only a few of you have ever had that ability, consider yourself blessed, for I consider myself blessed to know you." Blenadrene said as he gathered his thoughts.

Blenadrene then picked himself up and walked slowly towards the door with both hands on opposite walls to brace himself. The ship moaned with each lean from side to side. Blenadrene stopped halfway down the hall and spewed liquids from his mouth.

"Dinora," He called in his weak state, "Dinora."

She heard her master's voice and rushed to the door in her sleep clothes. She opened the door swiftly and saw him in front of her looking pale and sick.

"What is wrong, master?" she asked worried.

"There is no time to explain, there is more I need to show you, and there is not much time. We must go to the middle ship. Get dressed." The sick wizard demanded.

She went back in her room and closed the door. The ship took a deep dip in a wave that must have been huge, and again Blenadrene spilled fluids from his mouth.

"Ewww!" Mlar said as he watched attentively.

After a few moments, Dinora returned fully dressed. Blenadrene waved his hand and they both became smoke that floated to the nearest window and seeped through the cracks of it.

Mlar flew up to the window and watched the smoke dance through the air towards the middle ship. Deckhands on the ship watched as the smoke weaved through and around them before seeping through the deck, like spilled ale. Two decks below, the two materialized walking towards a door, looking like wood that was afire that water had just doused.

Blenadrene lead Dinora into a room that had a ten-inch thick wooden door. He waved his hand and the door opened as if an old man was pulling it from the other side.

"Enter, my pupil." said Blenadrene.

She walked in and felt a chill that was like ice.

There was a circle drawn on the floor with crushed oyster shells and a lone candle in the middle.

"What have we come here for, Master?" she asked.

"There is one more piece of magic I must show you before we get too close to Emolia. Sit." he said.

He motioned her to one side of the circle and he sat opposite of her.

He closed his eyes and then the candle's flame began to flutter sporadically causing the shadows in the room to shift as if they were alive. Then all of the sudden the flame stopped and began to grow taller. The color changed to a bright purple then flashed.

Dinora covered her eyes with her forearm as she leaned back.

The flash calmed into a purple glow that glazed the room over, and there was a calm presence.

Dinora took her arm from her face and saw what appeared to be a living diamond reach out to touch her. The being was beautiful and shimmered with the purple glow radiating off of its form. As the hand extended towards Dinora, it finally touched her forehead and the glow went from the being's hand and it turned to dust starting at its feet and ending at the fingertip that touched her, leaving a shard that sunk into Dinora's skin and disappeared. She was in a state of shock.

"Dinora, are you okay?" asked Blenadrene.

Through her eyes the room became bright and then she lost consciousness.

11

WHEN STEEL TOUCHES

I awoke to find all of his wounds had healed. He looked around to see the sun had risen and the jungle was very much alive with all sorts of animal inhabitants. The fire he lay next to was now being used to heat a small cauldron.

The weapons he saw before passing out were all clean and looked priceless. There were all styles of swords, bows, axes, staffs, clubs, hammers, bolos, throwing knives, armor, whips, and weapons I had never seen before.

There was one thing that caught I's attention and seemed to call out to him. There was a tall, bending staff that had a blade which looked as if it stabbed through the top of the staff; hung on its side by two golden hooks attached to a huge black tree. The blade curved down and it was as about as long as the staff. I reached out to touch it, and before he could feel the dark wood of the staff, there was a whooping noise that chopped through the air and caused I to duck instinctively.

Whop! A double-sided axe stuck into the side of the black tree right above I's head. He looked back to where the axe had come from and there stood the human woman.

She was dressed in a white garb and stood very tall and fair skinned. She resembled the angelic beings in books Blenadrene had read to I when he was little.

"You may not touch the Dragon's Tooth, for you are not worthy elf." She spoke with a look of the utmost sincerity. "All who have dared touched the Dragon's Tooth and are not worthy burst into flames and burn until nothing remains. Not even the blessed water of Lanteen can put out the fire!" the women said with the utmost confidence. "Come let your training begin!"

The beautiful woman tossed I a short sword and shield and told him to defend himself. She approached the young elf with battle hammer and a whip. She raised the hammer and brought it down towards I in such a way that he was barely able to get the shield up to take the blow.

Before I could get his stance steady, she again delivered blow after powerful blow against the shield and had I on his back. When he looked up, she was standing a few feet away and the hammer was in the air flipping towards him. I turned the shield up to deflect the hammer to the sky, only to feel the whip crack him across his stomach. I shrieked out in pain.

"I see your skin has some feeling left in it. Let us see what color the blotted one bleeds." she said.

She began cracking the whip at an amazing speed striking I all over the parts of his body the shield could not cover. The pain was excruciating.

"Defend yourself, or you will not live to save us young elf!" the white skinned woman proclaimed.

She began to crack the whip again and I was able to move the shield to block most of the strikes, but the ones that connected stung and drew blood.

"I will take the flesh off the bone with my next strike young one so you'd better be ready to defend or scream!" she yelled.

The whip came at I and he moved the sword in the way and watched the whip tangle around it, he then yanked the whip from the grasp of the human and tossed the shield at her.

She ducked the shield by going into a full split then she pulled her legs into the front of her sitting upright. She then she tucked and rolled backwards and stood but not before she grabbed two daggers from her boot and flung them at I.

He deflected both daggers with the sword and looked for the woman. She had picked up two katana blades and crept toward I twirling them.

"How long do you plan on holding that sword, elf?" she said with a smile.

"For as long as destiny says that I must." He replied.

"I have destiny's answer for you, child!" she all but laughed.

She charged I thrusting the blades up towards his neck.

He blocked with the sword one hand on the handle the other behind the blade, leaving both of their faces a breath from one another.

"You are a fast study, blotted one, but not fast enough!" she said.

She slid both blades outward upon the sword, cutting I's left hand and locking the sword's blade in with the blade she slid towards the right hand. She twisted both her blades and snapped the sword. Then she delivered a kick into the same spot in I's stomach that she popped with the whip.

The kick pushed I back into a weapon holder that housed metal fans with razor-sharp edges. He wielded two and became accustomed to their weight and movement almost instantly.

The human woman attacked again, and with every thrust, I was able to thwart her blades with the golden fans. She hurled both blades at I and he easily blocked them away into the jungle.

"I see that you have not forgotten, and your reflexes have gotten even quicker!!" she smiled.

She flipped over to a rack of staffs that varied in style and picked out a long silver staff, motioned it around her body, took a battle stance, and charged yet again.

The blotted elf stood his ground twirling the golden fans.

The beautiful human jumped into the air, popping the staff to reveal a chain in the middle and two hook type blades on each end. She landed spinning the weapon by the chain over her head, then flung one hooked rod then the other right after at I still holding the chain.

I blocked both the blades with the fans to his left side but the hooks had pierced the fans and the woman quickly yanked them from I's hands. She caught both sides of the staff in her hands and took anther battle stance.

"You know these weapons very well, fair human." The blotted elf said.

"As you also know, young elf." She responded.

"What is your name, skilled warrior?" I asked.

"Disarm me, and I shall tell you my name." She replied.

I looked upon all the weapons that were displayed and saw the staff the Orc had given him. He raised his hand and the staff came to him.

"The one with no name has freed your mind, I see." The human said mockingly as she charged again.

I waited patiently, twirling the staff as his attacker grew closer.

When she was close enough, she got low and slid into range for her attack. She swiped at I's legs, he blocked, she kicked, he blocked, she thrust forward, he blocked, she jumped to kick his face, he ducked.

The two went on for hours in awesome speed with her lunging and him blocking and dodging every attempt to strike him. Then with a swift motion, she kicked up dirt into I's face causing him to be blinded momentarily.

She flipped forward to deliver a blow with the hooked ends of the silver staff, and I on bended knee held the staff up in time to catch both hooks in the staff. She grabbed the chain in an attempt to disarm I, but his grip was to strong this time.

He then spun the staff quickly to snare her hands in the chain she was holding. He then pulled her to him in a mighty jerk, embracing her body tight so that their faces again where but a breath away from one another's.

She squirmed but I's strength was too much for her to break from.

"And your name, my fair lady, would be?" he smiled.

"Tleisha, boy elf, now release me if you truly value your arm!" she demanded as she struggled.

I did as Tleisha asked. She pushed him away bitterly.

"Rest now, elf, at dawn you will learn to attack!"

She walked to the other side of the fire. I walked to follow but she was gone. The young elf placed his staff against the black tree and walked over to the cauldron being warmed.

As he lifted the pot, he smelled stew that reminded him of his mother and he began to cry. He then remembered his mother's words of encouragement to be strong and return to her. He wiped his tears from his eyes, filled a small bowl of the stew, and began to eat. He thought of the happy times he had seen on the Pixie Island, and how violent and relentless the time had been since his leaving.

He then thought of what Lomerian Centorial had showed him in the fog and knew these times were necessary. After his meal, he lay next to his staff and slept.

12

COLD DREAM

I's sleep was deep and peaceful. This was the first honest rest he had gotten since being dropped in the sea off the shore of Omegasa. There was a light breeze and all was calm.

I then felt a cold wind that caused him to shake but he could not awaken. He then began to dream. He saw in the jungle around him hundreds of hideous creatures of demonic sort, no two looking the same. The creatures appeared to be converging on his sleeping body. Some walked towards the camp, others floated.

As his vision drew nearer to his sleeping body, he saw the five elders dressed in ceremonial garb standing with their backs to him facing the jungle. All were poised in battle stance.

I heard the howls of the creatures getting louder, the trees were bent and snapped, the fire turned from orange to a bright blue. He watched as each of the elders one by one moved into a different part of the jungle, the last being Tleisha.

"You will not die nor be taken from the world this night, elf?" and she too charged into the brush.

The dream felt as though I was able to touch it, but he could not awake.

The air got colder causing his shake to turn into a shiver. There were screams and battle cries coming from the jungle all around I. There were bright lights from spells being cast, fire being thrown, and sparks from metal clanging together. The ground rumbled from time to time, and the fire next to I's body rose higher with every passing moment. The dream had I sweating profusely as he continued convulsing on the ground where he laid.

The battle seemed to rage through the night, getting closer to the body of the chosen elf.

More screams of pain and horror came through the thick wood, trees began to collapse, and moans of the death filled the air. Even the smell of battle seemed as though it could be grasped by the sleeping elf.

The jungle became quiet and I saw the elders back out of their respective parts of the jungle, all one by one as they had gone in.

They were yelling out to one another, but I could not make out what they were saying, their faces said it all. Frustration, disgust, and even a hint of fear showed in their expressions. Each of them looked around frantically, checking to see where the next attack would come from.

Lomerian kneeled down beside the fire and began to chant ancient words and moved his hand as though drawing in the air. The four others waited to see what would come through the brush into the camp that housed the one who would save us all.

Hundreds of eyes began to light up the dark wood that encircled the camp. The moans started yet again.

Lomerian began to chant louder into the fire. The four others stood their ground, waiting on the onslaught that approached. I's body shook hard then stopped. The blue flame rose higher into the sky and turned completely white. Lomerian's chanting stopped, and he fell to his hands and knees, dripping sweat from his body and saliva from his mouth.

Blygor grunted as the first demon rushed into the camp. The great troll smashed its head wide open with his club and it fell dead.

Tleisha ran to Lomerian's side.

"Did it work?" she yelled.

Lomerian could not speak; he just pointed his shaking hand to the fire where the outline of a massive cloaked figure floated.

More demons rushed the campsite looking for the blotted elf.

Rune began to bash one after the other with two diamond hammers.

The blind Orc sliced through each of the intruders with a sleek wide bladed sword.

I wanted to awake and end this horrible nightmare but could not.

I looked back to the fire as his vision began to become clouded. He saw the figure step down out of the fire towards Lomerian, grabbing him by the neck to cause the wizard harm. Lomerian then pointed over to I with a strange look on his face. The cloaked figure dropped Lomerian then looked at I then around the camp. Tleisha could do nothing but gaze upon the awesome cloaked figure and point to the black tree.

The massive figure floated like a specter over to the tree and removed the Dragon's Tooth. The cloaked figure looked over towards I again, but the hood he wore showed no face and in a flash the being darted as a blur into the jungle leaving a beam of white light behind.

The demons began to cry and howl in pain. The monsters inside the camp rushed into the jungle to retaliate, only to scream as their minions before them had. There was white light shooting all through the jungle and the hundreds of eyes in the dark all began to disappear. In a flash, the blur came from the jungle followed by the white light into the fire. There was a muffled boom and I awoke.

He took a deep breath and saw a bright sun shining through the trees and a burnt out fire.

"Young, protector, you seem to be shaken. What troubles you?" asked Tleisha.

"I had a terrible dream while I slept, death seemed certain, but—" he was interrupted.

"Say no more, young one, death is certain, when is the question. Your dream is yours. Gather yourself. We must leave here." The human said.

I looked around and saw the jungle was broken and burned.

"Where the demons I saw real? Was my dream not one?" He quickly turned to the black tree and saw the weapon was missing.

"Where is the Dragon's Tooth?" he asked frantically.

"The rightful possessor came for it while you slept." She answered.

"I saw him in my dream as well, who is he?" he asked with his eyes wide.

"I do not know, boy! You will have to ask Lomerian Centurial about him." She answered impatiently.

"Why do we need to leave? Lomerian can just summon him again to keep the demons at bay, right?" the young elf continued to question her.

"No, young one, a spell of that magnitude would have cost any other wizard his very existence, the spell almost destroyed Lomerian! Those were no regular demons either boy, those where the infantry for the great beast. They symbolize the time of The Withering. It is upon us. We must get you to the Emolian Empire, so you can save us." She said with a slight hint of fear.

"What is the name of this great beast?" I asked.

"I do not know it, young one." She replied.

"Well then, what is The Withering?" the young elf asked yet another question.

"Lomerian Centurial will tell you of these things, he awaits us at the docks." She said as she rolled her eyes.

13

Docks of the Forgotten

The docks were old and smelled stale. There was a light fog that held very powerful magic. The wood creaked and cracked with every step the human and young warrior took. There were flocks of scavenger birds perched all about the high places. These birds were five times as big as any scavenger bird I had seen. The stale smell slowly turned into the smell of aged death.

"Where is Lomerian?" asked I.

"He is here. Continue your steps young one." She ordered.

The main dock where they were headed seemed to stretch out for what seemed to be thousands of feet. The wood was more rotted and broken the further along they went.

The fog was getting thicker. The scavenger birds were in a deeper number as they walked as well, some with blood on their beaks and feathers, others fighting over limbs and organs, of what appeared to be new death.

"What is this place, Tleisha?" he questioning continued.

"These are the forgotten docks of Omagasa. Blenadrene's spell encircled the island and covered these docks many years ago. This island was a pivotal position in every war fought in the waters. The location gave armadas the access to more than seven empires. When wars between any of these empires would come upon Xahmore` this island would be the first position battled for. It is in the sea all alone and is no more than three months journey from the mightiest empires in all of Xahmore`. These forgotten docks cover about as much area as the island itself." She said to the blotted elf.

"I've never heard talk of these docks." He said.

"These docks have not been used in over two hundred years, young one. There has not been a war between the empires that required water travel, and the inhabitants of this island had no use for such a vast structure. The island has few occupants and the rest are passing through running from bounty hunters or royal courts. Some take up refuge on the island, but these docks are of no use to any one unless there is war." She answered.

The two continued on their walk and fog became so thick, they could barely see the rotted wood they walked upon. The scavenger bird numbers deepened even more. They started to fly close to the two. Some even began to walk behind their guest.

The smell almost became too repulsive for I to breath in. There were screams of excruciating pain in the distance, and the birds called out, most fled in the direction where the screams came from.

The fog suddenly began to lighten and a weak voice spoke.

"I see that you have made it and without a moment to waste, I feel The Withering is almost upon Xahmore`. Keep walking to the end of the docks."

The fog became lighter but only around the blotted elf and the human woman. It remained thick in the distance. They could hear ships rocking back and forth in the water. They could also hear the moans of half-dead seamen being torn apart by the scavenger birds. As the fog became clear around I and Tleisha, they witnessed the birds darting back and forth in numbers that would make anyone uneasy to be there. The docks had become so tattered, the water was starting to cover the part they were walking on.

I turned around and saw hundreds of the scavengers waddling behind them, looking at the two like they would be the next meal. They continued until the water was right below their knees, when they could see a floating figure about a hundred paces in front of them. Lomerian was hovering with both legs crossed, wearing a red garb that only the most powerful wizards of the Yorenzana were permitted to wear. His long, grey hair remained still in the oceans strong wind. His cream-colored skin now seemed more wrinkled than before. He meditated with his ring and middle fingers pressed to his thumbs and his arms away from his body and bent slightly. His grey beard flowed from his face to his torso past his crossed legs.

"Master," spoke Tleisha, "we are here."

He then touched the six fingers he used to meditate together and bowed his head. His eyes opened to reveal whitened pupils, he lifted his head to the sky and stretched his arms far apart, and the fog moved away like it lived.

The sight was awesome. There were more ships on this side of the island than what Lomerian had shown I a month or so before. Thousands upon thousands of ships were all swallowed in Blenadrene's spell. Wrecked, abandoned, old, new, humongous, to single passenger vessels. I then saw the birds perched on all of these ships and understood how they had become so large and unafraid. They had been feeding off the dying and the dead for close to twenty years becoming accustomed to feasts of flesh.

Lomerian then motioned his hands forward. The water began to ripple and ships began to drift away. The sound of the docks past Lomerian cracking and falling into the sea could be heard and kept getting louder and louder.

The scavenger birds began to fly away in droves. In the fog I saw a massive outline moving in their direction. The fog divided to reveal the most glorious of the ships the fog had collected!

Lomerian stepped down from his meditative state.

"This will be your vessel for the journey to the Emolian Empire, The Glynasha." said Lomerian.

The sleek ship was brilliantly crafted from the cream-colored Nellghan tree. All metal workings were gold and shined like they were freshly polished. The cannons were many in number and large in size. The sails where massive and a crimson color, with a large golden dragon stitched into them. The helm was fit for an admiral, with a wheel that was carved from a giant pearl, and outlined in gold.

"This vessel will reach the empire's docks in less than a month. Its speed is unrivaled by any ship." said Lomerian. "Let us board quickly, we haven't much time."

Lomerian then moved his hands and said more ancient words. The bodies of the dead crew and the birds that were feeding on them burst into flames and burned until nothing remained of them.

The three then boarded the ship.

14

SUMMONED INTO DARKNESS

What waits in the darkness? Secrets that are our deepest fear will one day come out. How we fear to have light even slightly graze what hides in the dark. For some of us mercy is granted to keep our deepest woes covered. But there comes a time in which what lies in the dark must be seen again.

A deep voice boomed out into several dark tunnels until it reached the ears of who it was sent to summon.

"Praylonese!" the voice bellowed. "Come!"

The servant was sitting at a wooden desk writing down by candlelight. He calmly rolled up the scroll and placed it aside, sat back, took a long relaxing breath, rose from his comfortable chair, and picked up the candle and walked to the doorway. He whispered to the flame and it left the wick of the candle and flickered through the air to a torch and the fire engulfed it instantaneously. He released the candelabra and it glided back to his desk. He spoke to the torch and it came off the wall and positioned itself ten paces in front of him. He then stepped up onto the air and hovered down the corridor as the torch led the way. The light from the torch illuminated the winding arch-shaped halls.

As he got closer to the one that summoned him, strange creatures walked in the halls, some cower from the flame, while others looked at it as to worship. Then he reached a staircase that wound downward against the wall of what appeared to be a tower. When he reached the bottom, there where statues of beings in robes in a vast hall that lead to huge arching doorway. As he reached the doorway, the flame of the torch increased but was barely able to light the massive chamber. Praylonese took a knee with a bowed head.

"You called for me, master, what is thy bidding?" he asked humbly.

"A presence is close that has evaded me for near to a hundred years, and he has something that I want." said the voice in the darkness.

"Who is it master?" asked Praylonese.

"Blenadrene." The voice said with anger.

Praylonese looked up with a sinister grin.

"He is very powerful, my servant, but I feel he is in a weakened state, take four ships and bring him to me. He is in a small fleet approaching Emolia." The voice commanded.

"Shall I destroy the fleet master?" asked Praylonese.

"They are of no concern to me, do as you please." The voice said.

"Shall I take Emolian ships?" Praylonese asked with a grin on his face.

"Yes, that will provide a nice touch. When he sees the flags, he will know he has been sent for." answered the voice.

"What is it he possesses that you want master?" inquired Praylonese.

The flame rose on the torch and jumped to what seemed to be a hundred or so torches that lined the wall of the great room, lighting it to show hundreds of demons and possessed elves but still leaving darkness on the far side of the room.

"Just do as I say and bring me the wizard Blenadrene!" the voice yelled angrily.

"Yes, master." Praylonese responded quickly.

"And Praylonese…" the voice began.

"Yes, my lord?" he asked.

"Do not fail me!" the deep voice said calmly.

The flames died down and the torches all released their flames back into the one original Praylonese used to light his way.

The darkness was still filled with whispers and snarls of the demons and possessed elves.

"I will not master." Said Praylonese humbly as he backed out of the room hovering the same way he came.

The torch once again lit his way and what little light was in the great chamber soon dissipated into the corridor.

15

INSIDE THE GLYNASHA

I stepped onto the vessel and was taken by its beauty. The deck was a cold thin sheet of hard cream marble with a map of Xahmore` imprinted in gold. He awed in the size and detail of the impression. He then closed his eyes and listened to the sails that were attached to masts that bent back flap in the wind.

"This ship is forever yours when you need it, young one" said Rune who appeared from the stairs leading to the deck below, "There are things here you need to see, come."

I followed the massive dwarf who could barely fit through the wide door. Before he passed through the doorway, he looked up to see Lomerian hovering, his legs crossed in front of the pearl wheel. He turned the wheel without touching it to face the ship east. I heard a loud grunt and then saw Blygor pulling all the ropes at once to steady the sails and gather the wind that was about to be blown.

Lomerian spoke softly the word, "Wind."

By the thousands, all the birds flew away at once, the trees on the island looked as if a hand brushed over the top of them, the docks that were well rotted crumbled into the sea, and the vast number of ships that could be seen from behind the Glynasha began capsizing and breaking to bits. The sails caught the extreme gust and the Glynasha lifted to the top of the water so that only the very bottom touched the water and off the ship went. The island became but a dot in the distance in seconds.

"Yes!" shouted the blotted elf as he ran to the banister to look back. "Woohoo! Rune, you said this is mine?"

"Correct, young elf, but there is a price for such a vessel." Rune said.

"A price?" the blotted elf asked.

"Yes, one of many you have already paid. Now come and see the things I spoke of." The muscular dwarf said.

I walked down behind the dwarf three levels below the main deck into the middle of a great library.

"What place is this, Rune?" asked I.

"The Scribe's Den." He answered.

"How can this be? The den is located on the eastern most border of Emolia's provinces?" The young, well-studied elf asked.

"Look, young one, towards the end of the room." Rune pointed.

I looked and watched as books came off of and went back to the shelves. Some went to tables in the room and opened up, some left through different doorways.

"Emolia has the greatest source of collective magic in Xahmore` I," said Lomerian as he entered the Den. "this library contains a copy of every piece of literature in one place, but is magically linked to points in Xahmore` that scribes from Emolia can collect and record info and place it here for all who can walk into the den to see. The books you see are actually being read, returned, or happen to be new writings being placed here.

"Why is the den here if it is for the Emolian scribes only? Why would this ship be lost in the fog and is from the Emolian Empire? They would not come for me with evil intentions would they, Lomerian?" asked the young elf.

"There is evil in the most righteous of places, young one, and for this ship to be one that was lost in Blenadrene's fog means there is evil in high places in Emolia. All evil has done in this case was give you the knowledge and a vessel to complete the tasks at hand." said Rune.

"Come there is more to see, young elf." said Lomerian.

They walked through one of the doorways from the den and down another level into what appeared to be a weapons room. This room was vast and appeared to cover one of the whole lower decks on the ship. The walls were graced by head and shoulder paintings of elves. Each one of them looked regal. Their ears pointy, their faces without blemish, the fairest race was represented by male and female alike.

"Who are they, Rune?" asked I.

"These are the greatest warriors of your kind. Swordsmen, archers, beast masters, wizards, scouts, spirit holders, and so on. Some I have had the pleasure of knowing and others the honor of battling. I have a feeling you may know a few of them." Rune replied.

As I looked over the paintings, he realized he had seen all of the hundreds of faces before. He recalled them from dreams he had when he was younger. He had been visited by many of them ,and they had told him their stories. As he looked over more of the paintings, he saw that Lomerian's image was high upon the wall next to three others: a female spirit holder, an older male swords master, and another male who was a beast master.

"Rune, what is the significance of these four paintings being over all the rest?" asked I.

"These are the greatest warriors of all. They made the greatest of sacrifices for the elfin race, and they have been placed above all warriors as the model by which one defines himself as a hero." Rune answered.

I then looked and saw a vey familiar face, Blenadrene. He'd known Blenadrene was powerful, but one of the greatest elf warriors, no. He stood and stared at the picture until Rune placed his hands upon I's shoulder.

"Yes, your mother's mentor and your self-appointed protector. He could very well be on the wall next to Lomerian but had his differences with Emperor Telaris when it came to the war he waged against the Shamual." said Rune.

"The Shamual?" asked I inquisitively.

"Yes, they were a race of huge cats that walked on two legs and controlled the Crystal Mountains of Greyjohst, right on the edge of Telaris's growing empire. They had a particular crystal that Telaris wanted, Ulrant. It was said that at one time there were crystal beings and that the last one broke himself and placed a shard into the forehead of a huge cat and it created a new race, a race he taught everything he knew. The crystal being's name was Ulrant, the very crystal that Telaris wanted was his essence. The Shamual would not become one of Telaris's allies, and their leader, Muline, would not grant access to the magical crystal. The Shamual were the guardians of the magical crystal and knew that power in the wrong hands could be fatal to us all. The young emperor was enraged that all of his attempts to gain access to the crystal by civil means were turned down again and again by Muline. After hundreds of years of asking for an alliance, he called for an army lead by his greatest wizard to go and get the crystal. Blenadrene was that wizard. He pleaded with Telaris to leave the Shamual be, but he could not move the Emperor. The war over the crystal lasted ten years. Against all that he believed, Blenadrene walked into Muline's great chamber and demanded the crystal in the name of the emperor. The battle was one that will be told of until the end of us all. Before Blenadrene struck the last blow to finish Muline, the crystal shard illuminated and endowed Blenadrene with the knowledge passed from Ulrant to Muline. Blenadrene began to cry from the images and knowledge he was blessed with and the blow was never struck. Blenadrene looked around at all the death and destruction that he had been a part of and told his followers to leave and cast a spell that froze the entire mountaintop and made it so that anyone who stepped foot inside the great hall would freeze into ice. So the crystal remained safe. He never returned to the empire." said Rune.

"So it was destiny that we met on the island and not just chance. My mother hid for protection, he was hiding for solitude." The black-eyed elf said.

"Not only solitude, young elf, but hiding until his destiny led him back to Emolia. He had to find peace with all he had done in the name of the emperor and forgive himself before returning to face Telaris Emolian. There were many secrets revealed to Blenadrene when Muline gave him the visions of Ulrant." said Rune.

"What kind of secrets?" asked the young elf.

"I do not know but they must have been hideous to make arguably the greatest wizard repent and seek seclusion for over a hundred years. I guess time will show itself soon and the secrets he holds will be revealed for we get closer to Emolia every moment." The dwarf said.

16

UNEASY WATERS

As the sun began to rise in the far horizon, the water appeared to shimmer as emeralds in front of the lowly fleet from Omegasa. The wind blew mildly and the smell of the sea was pleasant. The usual hands were on deck performing the tasks of cleaning, catching and cleaning fish, and navigating the course to their destination. And then it all changed with the words from the lookout atop the flagship.

"Ships to the east, ships to the east." the lookout yelled to the captain.

The captain extended his telescope so that he could get a better look at the ships on the horizon. He surveyed the ships and witnessed the ships flew Emolian flags. There where four vessels with full crews and they were approaching fast. He looked closer and noticed that the crew was loading cannons and preparing for battle.

"Battle stations, these ships are Emolian battle vessels and are preparing for attack!" he commanded.

All hands scurried like mice to arm themselves, tie down loose items, and load cannons. The captain lifted his metal telescope to his eye to take in more of the oncoming fleet's actions. He noticed all the elves on the lead ship bow when an elf draped in a red robe stepped up on to the deck.

"Lord Praylonese, we have prepared to attack and await your command," said the captain of the Emolian flagship.

"Good, when we come within range, begin firing our cannons and do not stop." He ordered.

"Yes, my lord, as you wish." The captain replied.

Praylonese walked to the front of the ship and gazed out at the Omagasian fleet. He noticed a reflection of light coming from the main vessel. The captain of the Omagasian fleet noticed the elf in red looking directly at him through the telescope. The elf then smiled an evil smile and shook his index finger and head slightly at the captain. The captain was in shock and could not move the telescope from his eye. The elf then snapped his fingers and the glass on both sides of the telescope shattered.

"Agh…my eye!" screamed the captain as shards of glass sliced his face and eye.

The crew rushed to his aid.

"Captain, are we in range to fire yet?" asked Praylonese.

"No, my lord, we are still far out of range." He replied.

"Well then, in that case, let us see how well their ships can float."

Praylonese put his hands in a position as to lift something heavy. His eyes began to glow red and the water in between the two fleets became uneasy. He pulled his hands up and the water rose high so that neither fleet could see the other. He then motioned his hands forward and the water moved as huge wave.

As the wave approached, the force of it pushed wind across the deck of all the ships from Omegasa. The dedicated magicians and wizards from each ship stepped forth to counter the spell cast by Praylonese. Human, orc, pixie, elf, and halfling spell casters all stepped forward with their palms facing forward to dispel the wave, but could only slow it. The wind began to carry mist from the wave over the decks of the ships from Omegasa.

Praylonese chuckled to himself. And pushed his hands forward in a mighty thrust. The magic users on the other side of the wave were all knocked off of their feet, and one by one they fell and with them any chance of stopping the wave, as it began once again to roll closer. The crew just watched helplessly as the end approached.

Blenadrene sat in Dinora's company watching her toss and turn in her sleep. He felt the dark magical wave approach and waited until it touched the first ship and held his hand out not taking his eyes off of Dinora. The wave stopped with the first ship leaning slightly back.

Praylonese pushed as hard as he could to send the wave crashing onto the fleet but could not, Blenadrene was too strong.

Blenadrene leaned forward and kissed Dinora on her forehead.

"I will see you again, my heart, destiny will provide us the time for one another, but now I must protect you." said Blenadrene to Dinora as she kept tossing and turning.

He then thrust his hand forward and sent the wave back twice as fast as it was sent. He stood and walked out of the chamber where Dinora slept. Praylonese was in shock as the wave came back towards him. He tried to stop it and could not. The wave increased in size and the gust of wind now came over the Emolian ships. The wind began to rip their sails and Praylonese became furious. He began to pull the wave towards him even faster, and right as it was about to crash into the ships, he motioned his body so as to chop the air and split it in half then pushed his arms out sending the wave around both sides of the fleet. As it cleared the fleet, he swung both his arms around causing the halves to swing back around in front of the Emolian ships to rejoin and he pushed the wave back toward the oncoming fleet once again.

Blenadrene stepped up from below the deck still queasy and sick and took to the air. He flew over the top of the enormous wave as it reached the halfway point between fleets and caused it to crash upon itself back into the ocean.

Praylonese looked upon the great wizard floating over the sea in a brown tattered cloak. He clenched his teeth and took a running start from the deck to the banister and flew up to meet Blenadrene. The two hovered high above the water.

Blenadrene recognized the red robe the wizard wore, it was the robe of the Yorenzana enforcer only second in power to the High Wizard. So Blenadrene loosened his cloak and shed it into the sea to reveal a regal green robe trimmed in gold.

"Why do you attack us?" asked Blenadrene with authority.

"You may wear the high wizard's robe of the Yorenzana, but it is not recognized any longer." said Praylonese.

"Recognized or not, you should turn back before I am forced to destroy you all." threatened Blenadrene.

"I don't think so, I know you have great power, but my master has sent me to fetch you, you apparently have something he wants. Besides you don't look so well Blenadrene." said Praylonese.

"I am more than well enough to defeat you." proclaimed the high wizard.

"But can you defeat me and protect your people at the same time?" asked Praylonese.

And no sooner than the statement was made, the cannons from the Emolian ships blared like thunder unleashing an all out assault on the weary travelers from Omegasa. Blenadrene threw a lightning bolt into Praylonese chest, causing him to fall towards the water and turned his attention on the cannon balls headed toward the fleet.

The flaming pieces of metal were about to reach the ships when Blenadrene took control of them and redirected them back towards the lead Emolian vessel causing close to forty cannon balls to bombard the ship, destroying it. The remaining ships fired again, but Blenadrene was too weak to perform the same spell, so he decided to protect the middle ship.

"Return fire!" he yelled to the ships from Omegasa.

They did as he commanded. The ships in the battle were all being hit and torn apart, all except the middle ship that Blenadrene was protecting. Thwarting cannon ball after cannon ball, he weakened more with every spell. He was sweating and holding on with nothing but the love for his adopted pupil. Without warning, he was swallowed by a sphere of water and looked to see Praylonese hovering through smoke caused by a fire coming from burning debris. His robe and chest were burned by the bolt Blenadrene had struck him with earlier. His eyes red with anger, he spoke.

"I have you now, why don't you take a deep breath?" said Praylonese.

Weary and tired Blenadrene smiled at Praylonese and did just that. With one deep continuous breath Blenadrene inhaled all the water from his wet cage.

Praylonese was astonished.

Blenadrene then exhaled a mist so cold that when it reached Praylonese it froze his left hand as he extended it to block the spell.

"Aagh!" Praylonese screamed as he grabbed his hand.

Then to Blenadrene's dismay, thinking he had stopped Praylonese, Praylonese smashed his frozen limb and spoke dark words over his arm and a new hand grew from his flesh, bone, and nerves and replaced the old. He looked towards Blenadrene and smiled.

"Creator, please help me." Blenadrene whispered into the atmosphere as Praylonese flexed his new limb and continued his attack.

The two floated back and forth in the sky trading spells and trying tricks to ensnare one another. Whenever he could Blenadrene shielded the ship holding Dinora, but his strength was fading fast and he could not hold on much longer.

17

WITNESSES OF LEGEND

I stayed between the weapons room and the great hall perfecting his skills and sharpening his mind. He had just about covered all the history of the elfin race and was astonished with double swords and staff. Tleisha could not contest him with either weapon and she had begun to help him master throwing spikes.

After about two weeks of travel and more than half the distance to Emolia covered, Blygor yelled for the crew to come top side. As they came to the deck, they saw smoke in the distance dead ahead. The awesome speed at which they had been traveling brought them up on what appeared to be a battle.

"Should we go around it, wise elder?" I asked Lomerian.

"This is not a battle we can or should avoid, young elf. Look again." Lomerian said as he pointed into the sea.

I looked out into the vast sea and saw what appeared to be two figures floating back and forth in the sky while ships fired cannons at one another. The two figures looked as if they were throwing lightning at each other while they flew at and away from one another. As the speedy vessel that carried I got even closer, he realized this battle was between the ships from Omegasa and ships flying red flags with dragons on them. Emolian ships, but why? Before I could even think about the questions, his ship was close enough to smell the gunpowder and hear the battle cries.

He looked back to the five elders to see Lomerian give him a nod as to say go and help. I then looked again to the battle and saw that it was Blenadrene in the sky battling another wizard. I could only think of his mother and where she was. He grabbed his staff and in the blink of an eye was over the edge of the ship running on the top of the water into the battle.

The speed at which he moved caused the water he crossed to gather behind him. He came to the first Emolian ship and leaped onto the deck with water behind him, smashing into the side of the ship, almost causing it to capsize.

"What is the meaning of this?" asked the blotted elf.

The entire crew stared in awe, as the world was seeing prophecy revealed. They all fell upon their faces.

"It is him, look at his eyes!" one said as they all bowed.

"Traitors, you only kneel before the Emperor!" shouted a voice from the sky.

I turned to see that Blenadrene had been lassoed by a red energy emitting from the other wizard's hand.

"Die for your betrayal!" screamed the wizard as he threw a bolt of energy from his free hand.

The bolt crackled in the air as it traveled toward the ship. I jumped right as the bolt hit the ship and blew it to bits. I jumped from piece to piece of the flying debris until he was on a massive piece that rose high enough to put him in between the powerful wizard and Blenadrene. He then reached out grabbed the wizard's lasso and snapped the red energy that ensnared Blenadrene before the huge piece of wood he was on began its downward decent. He then caught Blenadrene before he fell to the water and landed on the next Emolian ship. They too fell upon their faces. I proceeded to jump to the deck of every ship until the attack from the Emolian ships ended. Praylonese then descended to the same ship that I was on.

"Why have you attacked my people?" asked I.

The wizard draped in the red robe of the Yorenzana answered, "Your people are harboring a fugitive wanted by the Emperor himself, making them enemies of Emolia as well."

"They are no enemies of Emolia! Leave them be or die!" demanded I.

"I know who you are, blotted elf, but even you are not above the laws that govern all elves. Blenadrene must be punished and you will be punished with him if you do not turn him over to me. Give me Blenadrene and you all will be spared, resist and you all will perish." ordered Praylonese.

"I will not give you Blenadrene! Leave us be!" said I.

"You are strong, boy, but not yet strong enough to match me. I was not asking your permission, but giving you a chance to save lives." The wizard said with a grin and a laughed as he flexed his left hand.

"I will go." Blenadrene spoke.

"No." replied I.

"I must, it is my destiny." Blenadrene put his hand on I's shoulder and convinced I that it was the right thing to do. I agreed. "Besides, your mother should be waking from her nap shortly, she will be very pleased to see you."

"I don't agree, Blenadrene, but I will honor your decision. Wizard, tell our leader I will be there…soon." said I.

The red wizard with one swoop of his hand across the air caused himself and Blenadrene to fade away. "I am sure the ruler of Emolia already knows you are near, young elf, he already knows."

18

REUNION

I looked over the battle scene from the lead ship of the islanders and saw unnecessary death and destruction. Bodies floated in the water, one ship from each side was burning with flame, and smoke still consuming the hulls. Only two ships from the Omagasian fleet were still able to travel.

In the most turbulent time thus far in the journey, the people from Omegasa cheered for their young elf as the Emolian ships turned and left. He looked out over the cheering crowd with mixed emotions. Why would the elves attack in this way? Why did the wizard not receive him as graciously as the shipmen? Why did Blenadrene surrender? Why would the elves then leave without offering help?

In mid-contemplation he heard a familiar voice call out to him. "I, I, is that you?" shouted Mlar with excitement.

"Yes, Mlar." I replied with his emotions still out of balance.

"You look different. It has only been a few months and your physique has become larger, and your hair is now on your face. The way you moved was amazing just now. How did you do that?" ask Mlar.

"A freed mind, courage, and a trained body, but enough about that, how have you been, my friend?" I said.

"I've been well. I've been training a bit myself. Watch this." The pixie floated down to a hole in the deck of the ship and whistled. A large snake rose up and moved as he commanded.

"Amazing, you can talk to animals?" I said with astonishment.

"Yes, it is amazing. I thought I was about to be her dinner one day and she just stared at me. I talked and she understood." said Mlar.

"Incredible!" said the blotted black-eyed elf.

"I know. I still cannot believe I can do this!" said Mlar.

"I need to see my mother, is she alright, where is she?" asked I with concern.

"Blenadrene hid her on the middle ship when she passed out after one of their training sessions. She has been asleep for a few days." replied Mlar.

"Take me to her." I said to his friend.

The middle ship was the boat that housed all of the most prized possessions of the islanders. The boat was made of a thick dark wood that could withstand ramming from another ship and small cannon balls. Mlar led I below deck to where his mother laid asleep. I walked into the room. The candlelight flickered in the room, waving light over her beautiful face. I stood there glad to see his mother.

"Mother," he whispered, "please, wake up."

Her eyes opened quickly, as she gasped for a deep breath and started to breathe fast as if to wake from a nightmare.

"Mother, what is wrong?" he asked.

"Son, there is danger in Emolia. Danger like the world has never seen, where is Blenadrene?" she asked frantically.

"He was taken by an Emolian wizard." Her son answered.

"We must find him. All of Emolia will be graves, if we do not!" Dinora said.

"What danger, mother? What is wrong?" I asked.

"Things are not as they appear. Blenadrene shared a vision of the past with me. There is very dark magic enshrouding the empire, we must move quickly!"

I grabbed his mother and Mlar and hurried back to the Glynasha.

Dinora stepped to the bow of the magnificent ship and addressed all the Omagasians.

"All of you that are warriors, wizards, or have any special skills, take care of the ones who do not. Harsh times are upon us and we must make sure we survive if at all possible. Do not go to Emolia for death awaits. Dock south of Emolia, and we will send word when it is safe to enter the Empire of the Elves."

She stepped down and looked at her son with tears in her eyes.

"I fear I will never hold you again as a mother, for the days ahead we will both be warriors, and these days will outlast the lives of most."

She then hugged her son with an embrace as if she wanted to become a part of him.

"We must go now." she ordered.

"Go below deck, mother. Mlar, go with her, I'll be there shortly." I told his loved ones.

I looked up to the helm to see Lomerian floating by the pearl wheel. He looked to the sails to see Blygor bracing the ropes. He then looked to see Rune standing right next to him. He looked to the night sky behind him where the two moons' light peered from behind the clouds. The clouds suddenly dispersed and I thought, *wind*. The Glynasha's sails where filled and the vessel darted off towards Emolia, towards unknown evil, towards death.

19

CAPTIVE OF THE DARK

In a temple with no location, voices conspired in the darkness among dim torches and water leaking through the cracks in between stone. Screams of terror engulfed the corridors. From nowhere there was a red light that flashed and showed Praylonese and a subdued being in front of his master, within the vast chamber of demons and possessed elves.

He lit the area close to him and Blenadrene with a energy radiating from his right hand.

"Master I have Blenadrene." Praylonese said proudly.

"Goooooooood!" his master said pleased.

In a motion of his hand, Praylonese moved the sickly Blenadrene in front of him bound wrist and feet by a red energy spell.

"Blenadrene, it is good to see you again." said the voice in the dark.

"I have never seen you, and if I had I would not have been your pawn." proclaimed the wizard.

"Ahhh, but you served me well, as well as your race. You helped build the greatest empire Xahmore` has ever seen with your powerful magic." taunted the voice in the dark.

"I served the emperor, not you, demon!" yelled Blenadrene.

"Yes, you did serve your emperor, Telaris, well. Ha, ha, ha, thank you for being his loyal subject, ha, ha, ha, ha!

Now if you would please give me what you were given by Muline, our business will be done." demanded the voice in the dark.

"It would serve my soul better to die!" said the wizard with conviction.

"Very well, Praylonese take him and pry it from him, painfully." commanded the voice in the dark.

"As you wish, master." replied the wizard in red.

Praylonese stepped up onto the air and floated out of the vast hall, lighting the way with his hand. Two demons then appeared from the darkness and began to drag Blenadrene behind the red wizard. They panted and grunted as they moved the wizard. They moved through many corridors before they stopped at a double door that had a huge plank holding it shut. The demons' panting stopped.

"You know, you should have just given him what he wants then he may have let you be a pet like he has the others." said Praylonese as he looked into the gold railing of the door and saw a reflection of Blenadrene holding the two demons' heads with a malicious look on his face and a green glow start to appear in his eye.

"Feeling better, are we?" Praylonese said mockingly, as he removed the plank with a wave of his hand.

The doors flung open and what appeared to be hundreds of chains that moved as if they lived entangled Blenadrene and snatched him into room.

Praylonese calmly followed and the door shut behind him.

20

SPIRIT OF ABANDONMENT

I walked about the ship looking for his mother to find her in the scribe's den asleep on a huge book.

"Mother, wake up, we are almost in Emolian waters." He said with a somber tone.

"Alright, my dear son, looks as though I studied until I could no more," she chuckled.

I did not smile.

"Tell me, was your journey to this point hard, son?" she asked as a concerned mother.

"It was necessary, mother." He answered as an obedient son.

"It will be no easier, I." she spoke to assure and make him aware.

"I know, mother, Lomerian and the others have warned me, trained me, and endowed me with the knowledge of the times we face. I know there is evil in high places. I know the Withering is upon us, and I know that existence itself is depending on me." he said to let her respectfully know he was no longer ignorant to the world around him.

"Well for as long as allowed, it will depend on us all." she said as his elder.

"What is it you are reading?" asked I.

"It is the history of it all. I am trying to study the nature of the beast." she replied.

"What do you mean the nature of beasts? There is no secret to the ways of beasts." He asked.

"No, my son, not just any beast. The great beast, the beast that is not animal but evil." she enlightened.

"Does this beast have a name?" I asked.

"It does but it is marked out of this book. The name is powerful enough to bring death upon those who say it, if they are not strong enough. And if you are strong enough, the name may summon one of his minions to destroy all around who said the name, so not everyone is allowed to know the name." she said.

"So what have you discovered thus far?" I asked.

"That the beast has been here from the start of our world, he was the creator's first bearer of life. He was not always evil but his evil was spawned by jealousy and envy of the elves. All beings were given a purpose and found favor with the creator. The creator loved us and found joy in our works. The beast, feeling as if he was forgotten, rebelled for the attention of the creator like a neglected child by using his power to deceive and cause the world to kill and betray, and fight for power that is not theirs, which is but a mere illusion. And he only shows his true self when he means to change the world for the utmost worst." she said.

"Well, if he hates us so and is so great, why does he not destroy us?" I asked.

"He does not destroy us all because he is not allowed to and he needs us to survive. Without us, he has no energy to feed upon." she answered.

"Why is he not allowed? What or who has the power to deny the great beast from doing what he feels?" I asked.

"The one that created it all." she smiled as she replied.

"Why doesn't the one who created it all stop this from happening? Let's find the one and ask for his help." the young elf asked and suggested.

"The one that created it all just watches and only intervenes when his chosen cannot carry on. The one does not manifest physically but shows through the events caused." she taught.

"We need the creator's help now. The Withering is upon us. The Emolian Empire has traces of evil throughout, and our friends are in grave danger!" I said with urgency.

"The one who created it all has helped us my son." Dinora reached out to touch her son's face. "You will protect us from the evils of the time. You will defeat this great beast when the moment is right. You were created by events that were caused, so you are the creator's help to us."

Just as I's mind began to wrap around what his mother had just spoken to him Mlar flew into the scribe's den with excitement in his eyes!

"I, you must come on deck and see, it is brilliant!" Then as quick as he flew in, he darted back the way he came.

Within two shakes of a red cat's tail I was on deck. The view was awesome! The night sky was lit up by the lights of the docks of Emolia. The buildings were tall marble, ivory, gold, and other textures I had never seen. The light came from lit torches and magic bulbs of various colors. The sky seemed to wave in the light. The illumination stretched down the coastline as far as one could see.

"Isn't it beautiful?" asked Mlar.

I was speechless. He had never seen such a sight in his life. The docks had thousands of boats docking, and torches and bulbs moved about looking like fireflies from the

Glynasha. Blygor lifted the sails and the ship slowed to a stop upon the calm waters.

"We will back away from land and return here in the morning." said Rune. "Lomerian would like to speak with you in the far corner of the scribe's den."

I then remembered that in those beautiful lights and magnificent architecture was a great and powerful evil, he then turned and walked back below deck.

He entered the den to see his mother still reading from the big black book. Then he looked into the far corner where Lomerian sat in the air one leg over the other meditating.

21

DISCOVERIES

Praylonese walked into the room of stone and chain, and he looked to the ceiling where five thick chains crossed over Blenadrene's head, chest, pelvis, knees, and ankles, pinning him there high on the sky. Thirteen demons stood guard under the great wizard.

"Fool, you do not even know what you are looking for!" said Blenadrene.

"You are wrong, high wizard, all the torture you have endured was for the punishment of running. I found it funny after my master told me where I can find what he seeks, so now I will pull it from your mind!"

Knowing he could not let the red wizard search his mind, Blenadrene summoned all that he had left to make a final attempted at freedom. He caused the chains to loosen, so that he could slip free and fall to the floor. As he landed on one knee, he touched the floor with his right hand and caused the stone floor to ripple as if he were a boulder thrown into a small pond. All the demons where smashed against the wall dead. Praylonese gracefully walked over the waving stone to wind up face to face with Blenadrene yet again.

"You have nothing left, high wizard." said Praylonese mockingly.

"But you do." said Blenadrene as he reached out and grabbed Praylonese by the face.

Blenadrene's eyes began to glow green, and he breathed in very slowly through his mouth. Praylonese screamed out in pain. Blenadrene was sucking the very energy from him. Before Blenadrene could siphon enough energy to fight his way to freedom, the deep voice boomed throughout the temple once again speaking an ancient demonic tongue. Brown cloth strips then came from the ground and wrapped Blenadrene's wrists and snatched them from the red wizard's face. More strips ensnared his feet holding him in place. He struggled to free himself but could not. Then numerous cloth strips came from the hole he had left and snatched him down to the ground and mummified him up to his neck. The strips then snatched him from his feet to his back slamming him harshly to the floor.

"Now, pull it from his head and bring it to me!" said the voice in the darkness.

Blenadrene spoke ancient words of his own into the air that sketched into the air and fell upon his forehead. Praylonese then reached into Blenadrene's mind causing Blenadrene to scream in agony.

An hour later Praylonese returned to the great chamber with blood on both his hands and a fearful look in his eye.

"Master, what will you have me do? Blenadrene does not possess what we seek." spoke Praylonese submissively.

His master then glanced into his mind to see if he was lying and found that he was not but did find an even more valuable piece of information.

"Where have you hidden it, Blenadrene? No worries, prepare him for the Washta. Nothing can stand in the way of the days to come. They have been prophesized. It will come to me!" said the booming voice in the darkness.

The dark voice paused for a moment then asked.

"Hmmm. Why did you not tell me you saw the black-eyed elf, Praylonese? And he is very close. There will be a fleet of ships waiting for you at the docks, use whatever force is necessary. He can not yet reach the throne before I have Ulrant."

"I will do as you command, master." The wizard said as he turned to leave.

"Do not underestimate him. He has more than just him and the two you see on his side. He has been blessed beyond comparison and must not be taken lightly." said the voice in the darkness.

"I understand, master." answered Praylonese.

"Do you? How was one who is not a wizard able to break your binding spell with ease? You must have been shocked. Hmmmm…slightly scared even. Why did you not destroy him then? Unsure of the extent of his power were you?" the voice in the dark then chuckled.

"I will deal with the travelers aboard the Glynasha." said the lesser being with shameful anger.

The dominant being's mood then changed and his eyes left the subordinate in front of him and moved to the side.

"Ahhhhh…I know you are there, old friend, you are not welcome in these walls anymore. I will permit you to leave now. Do so or you will cease to exist before your day." said the deep voice to a third party. "Tell the hero that he will know what it is to die before he can be victorious." Then the being released a vehement laugh.

The torches rose to a bright blaze as the laughter got louder. The lesser being arose and backed from the room. The laughter spread throughout the corridors of stone and darkness.

22

ELDERS' CONCERN

"What is it you wanted to speak to me about, Lomerian?" asked the black-eyed blotted elf.

"Yes, I, when the sun rises we will be greeted by an Emolian fleet, and they will attempt to hold us from the docks, and we must reach Telaris Emolian's throne room as soon as we can!" Lomerian said.

"Why is it so dire we reach the throne room as soon as we can?" asked I.

"The Beast, I fear he will enter back into our world from where he was trapped long ago by the dragons, beneath the place where the throne room was built. They are looking for something they thought Blenadrene had that may have something to do with the beast returning. We must reach the throne at all cost to prevent this, or the Withering will begin soon." Lomerian answered.

"Why halt his coming, I can defeat him!" said the young elf.

"Young elf, no one is yet strong enough to defeat the great beast. Did you not hear me say that the dragons imprisoned him? It took all of them, and many of them died in doing so. Some of us will be lost at his very appearance, but know you will not be. You will gain great power at a great price at the start of the Withering. Persevere." explained Lomerian.

"What about Blenadrene?" I asked concerned about his father figure.

"Blenadrene has been tortured horribly, and I fear he may be near his death." Lomerian said with great sadness.

"This is all so much to bear, Lomerian, how can I—" I began to complain but was interrupted.

"You must! You will find a way, you must not let the beast win!" proclaimed the great wizard. He looked at I with tears beginning to well and spoke, "Go and be with your mother, young elf." Lomerian commanded.

23

A Mother's Wisdom

I walked over to his mother and everything seemed to move slow as he watched her reading frantically from the big black book. As he got closer, he could see his mother's eyes were a bright blue and illuminated.

"Mother," I cried out, "What kind of magic is this?"

She looked up at her son and smiled and spoke, "Fret not, I, all is well. This is a spell that Blenadrene had not taught me yet." She closed her eyes and reopened them to show her beautiful grays. "It will allow me to use my soul's power to cast spells.

"That will be dangerous, surely the beings that posses that power can die!" I said.

"I was trained to have no fear, even if my life is at stake. If the beast or any of his minions is the threat, I would give my life in turn for what I call mine!" she said.

"It is my job to protect Xahmore` from such threats!" he stated.

"It is my job to protect my son from the harm that I can! There is more to being a warrior than the gain of victory, you must be willing to accept there will be loss and suffering before a war is won. You must also accept the fact that when you engage in battle, there is a chance you will become a legend in someone's stories instead of living to tell them yourself. I have accepted this fact, my son, you must do the same or you will never be able to protect anyone!" she countered.

"I don't plan on letting anyone fall in battle." The young elf said.

"These plans are not yours I. The actions you take are yours, but destiny cannot be ignored or denied, nor can it be changed." Dinora stated wisely.

"Then what good are my abilities and this power that I will gain if I cannot use it to protect the ones I love?" the young elf asked.

"The ones you love are not the only ones who need to be saved, my son. There are places where evil dwells, and you will be the only one who can stop it. There will be many lives you save, but you cannot save them all, some are destined to perish." she explained.

She could see the frustration on his face, so she stretched forth her arms. He slowly walked into her embrace as thoughts of his younger years raced through his mind. She pulled him in close. She is still slightly taller than her son as she pressed his head to her chest and kissed him atop his head. Then I heard a female's voice call to him.

"I come. I have something to give you." Tleisha called out.

"Mother, I must go. I love you." I said as he darted off.

"And I you, my son, go, I have one more spell to learn and I will see you when the sun rises." she said as she looked back into the book.

24

CLOTH AND DIAMOND

I walked into the great weapon's room. Past the numerous weapon racks, there was a wooden door in front of which stood Tleisha. She motioned for I to follow her as she walked through the door. I opened it to see a room that had numerous garbs and arms.

In the front of the room, there were nine distinct pieces of clothing that were draped on porcelain statues without faces.

"Stand and let what you need come to you." said Tleisha.

I walked into the middle of the room, closed his eyes, and leaned his head back. He released a deep breath and his clothes fell from him to the floor. He felt a very powerful presence come into the room, but it could not be seen.

The garbs and armor lifted from their resting places and began to float around the room at a frantic pace orbiting I in a sphere. He felt new clothing being strapped onto him made of leather and the finest of cloth. No armor and everything black.

His boots were as light as air. His forearms were covered with assassin's bracelets that left about seven inches of strap hanging from his wrist. These over time would become his favorite things. His torso was covered by a thick piece of leather under what appeared to be a modified robe of the Yorenzana, which left his arms exposed and came up to his jawbone. Its form fit his thin muscular frame up to his waist, where it then draped as a regular robe but was split from the floor in front back and sides to allow free movement of his legs. His pants where baggy and made of a fine cloth material and tucked into his boots. Around his waist was a strap that held seven silver stakes on his right side. The frantic pace of the orbiting attire stopped, and I stood there in front of the nine statues. All of them were now bowing before him, except one.

There was a statue that wore a black cloak that walked up to I and placed its hand on I's shoulder. The statue took the shape of I and then manifested his face where there was not one. The statue removed the cloak and kneeled down before I with it stretched forth to him. I reached down for the cloak, and it quickly draped itself onto him. He removed the hood of the thick cloak and it disappeared. The statue of I then stood and turned to face the bowing statues and raised a hand in victory and ceased to move once more.

The room became quite then the human woman spoke.

"Young elf, there is one more gift that is yours." said Tleisha. "Come."

They entered back into the weapon's chamber where Rune, Blygor, Lomerian, and the Orc with no name waited.

"There young elf, on the wall at the far end of the chamber," announced Rune,"The Swords of Jahmbesha!"

I walked to the wall that held the sheathed swords. They were hanging on a stone disc that had an impression of a dragon's head spitting fire. He removed the swords from the wall to feel they were very heavy, but nothing he could not handle. He removed one of the swords from its sheath to see the blade was a black diamond. The diamond blade was a fine point that became a wide blade that went out to two more points then cascaded from wide to slim until it reached the white handles with dark red rubies at the back of both.

"How is this possible?" asked I.

"The blades were forged in dragon's fire by a graphite being, Jahmbesha, who was the greatest weapons smith of all time. The dwarf weapons smiths envied him. The dragon asked Jahmbesha to forge the sword out of a black diamond he brought to Jahmbesha. Only the dragon's breath was hot enough to make the diamond manageable for Jahmbesha to mold. The heat generated by the dragon also took Jahmbesha's life in the process. Irony, his greatest work, and he never even saw it completed. After the blades were forged, the dragon attached the handles Jahmbesha had made. I trained you on how to use these when you were but six. It will all come back when you draw your blades for battle." said Tleisha.

"What will I remember? How did they wind up here? who was the dragon?" asked I.

"Answers that will have to be found another day, young elf, it is time." she said.

I strapped the sheaths over opposite shoulders and walked out behind the elders, onto the deck where his mother and Mlar were waiting at the front of the ship, looking out onto the water.

The sun was bright and hot. There was no wind. When I reached the front of the ship, he saw the large armada that had been sent to meet them. I looked to the bow of the flagship and there stood the red-bearded wizard with a smile on his face.

The wizard said in a sinister tone, "Welcome to the Emolian Empire, we've been expecting you!"

25

PROTECTOR REVEALED

It seemed as if all time stood still; there was no breeze, no waves, not even a single bird in the sky. The docks of Emolia were just a few miles past the horizon. All parties involved stood still waiting, and then I spoke.

"We wish an audience with the emperor." yelled I to the red-bearded wizard as he studied the formation of the hundred or so ships before him.

In his study, he noticed that the shipmen's eyes were bright red, unlike the ones he had encountered before. He knew a dark magic was in play.

"The only audience you will be having is with me and then with the depths of the sea, young elf, if you do not turn over yourself and your crew to us." The wizard replied.

"We shall not surrender, destiny has lead us this far. I have come to speak with the ruler of the elves and to free my friend, red one!" I said mockingly as he stepped out to the tip of the long slim bow making him an easy target.

"My name is Praylonese, and the red that will be remembered this day is the blood that spilled into these waters." The wizard raised his arms as to signal an attack.

I looked back at his mother and friend and then to the elders.

"A little help, please." I said as he smiled then dropped down from the bow and began to run on the sea surface, dragging his staff behind in the water.

There was a loud boom and gust as he ran by the Emolian warships blowing those on deck off their feet and causing the boats to rock in the deep waters.

"You coward, you run and leave your vessel and companions for slaughter?" the wizard proclaimed as he dropped his hands to begin the attack.

Cannons blared, arrows darkened the sky, and war cries came from all of the Emolian ships.

As all the shrapnel and arrows floated towards the Glynasha, the water where I dragged his staff began to separate causing the Glynasha to tip into a one hundred foot deep channel. A spell then pushed wind into the sails for a slight boost into the channel. The ship declined into the split at an amazing speed that was maintained by the water closing behind it and the wind spell provided a push.

All metal and arrows fell into the sea, as the Glynasha sailed through the armada. The warships on the sides of the Glynasha tried to fire on it but to no avail. Some even obliterated other warships with cannon fire in their attempts to stop the Glynasha. As the water closed behind the vessel, the warships on each side were smashed into one another causing them to sink.

Before Praylonese's ship was sucked into the channel, he cast a spell pulling the flagship out of the water and in pursuit of the Glynasha by air. He positioned the ship a few hundred feet above the Glynasha and began to hurl fireballs at the vessel.

Mlar noticed the ship approaching and alerted Dinora. Just before the first massive crackling ball of fire struck, she cast a spell using the surrounding water to destroy it. There was an explosion then a hiss as the water evaporated from every fireball he threw, which she destroyed.

Praylonese was not pleased and began to chant angrily, the sky became dark with clouds that illuminated with lightning.

Mlar looked into the sea and observed the marine life had become very active due to the events taking place. He noticed a huge sea serpent moving about in the clear waters and began calling to it.

"Come to my aid, great serpent, come to my aid" Mlar repeated with his eye fixated on the water creature.

The creature then looked back at Mlar. Without a moment's delay, the serpent jolted straight up at the flagship Praylonese commanded and smashed into the bottom of it, creating a huge hole and breaking the spell holding it in the air.

Praylonese's concentration had been broken. The sky returned to normal as Praylonese was forced to levitate himself from the falling boat. By the time he regained sight of the Glynasha, it had almost reached the coastline of Emolia.

He let out a menacing cry into the air then, spoke "Master, I have not failed you yet." He waved his hand and disappeared yet again.

I realized his crew was out of the range of the Emolian ships and that Praylonese had given up his pursuit, so he pulled the staff from the water and leaped straight into the air. As the Glynasha came to the end of the channel, it was forced upward by the water closing in front of it, causing it to jump from the channel and skip across the water.

"What a ride!" proclaimed Mlar excitedly face down on the deck.

Once Dinora and Mlar gained their footing, I landed on the deck with his staff in hand and on a bended knee facing his mother.

"Forgive me, mother, for making such a brash decision without alerting you, but I did not want you to be taken or harmed as Blenadrene was." I said with the emotion of sadness in his voice.

She ran over to the young elf and collapsed to put her arms around him.

"You did brilliantly, my help from the creator, of all, my son, you did brilliantly!" she said overjoyed.

The Glynasha's force carried it the rest of the journey, easing it into the docks where there was a crowd that watched the entire episode unfold at sea. As the Glynasha docked, the crowd cheered with great excitement. Mlar stepped off first followed by Dinora then I.

When the elves at the docks saw the eyes of I, all bowed with one knee and made a path for the newcomers. They walked through the path that was made by the crowd. Every step they took, more elves bowed to a knee.

Then there was one elf in the middle of the path, he too was a blotted elf, very old and was scarred horribly. He propped his pain-ridden, yet muscular body up on a self-made wooden crutch. His beard was matted and grey and patchy. He stretched forth his hand nervously pointing his shaky finger at I.

"Is it you? Have you finally come to help us all? I have so long waited for this day, please tell me it is you!" his ragged old voice pleaded. "Are you the black-eyed blotted elf that legend speaks of?"

I looked out over the crowd as they looked back with the anticipation of his answer.

"Yes, I am!" I proclaimed.

The crowed rose up with a great roar of delight! There were whispers in the crowd as all the onlookers pointed and began to converse about the events that had transpired and those to come.

The old elf then hobbled forth and asked, "Is there anything I can do for you, protector?"

"Yes, there is old one, first tell me your name." I requested.

"Rimleon, my lord." the old elf answered.

"Well Rimleon, my friend," said I in a deep, almost angered tone as he placed his hand on the old elf's shoulder, "Take me to the emperor!"

26

MISLEAD

Inside the palace there was a familiar face and voice that rang out in anger!

"Back away from me and let me in to see Telaris Emolian!!" the voice demanded.

Two guards held their tall scepters to block the intruder as one spoke.

"You will call him emperor, wizard!" one of the guards said.

"We will call you dead, if you do not open those doors. I shall open them myself before your body hits the ground," the wizard said.

The guards opened the huge golden doors hurriedly! The brightness of the next room illuminated the dark hall that led to it.

The wizard entered into a vast throne room where there was soft music from a harp, chimes, and a beautiful voice singing just as soft over it. The entire throne room was white marble with gold that trimmed every streamline and corner. The ceiling was so high; it appeared to be unreachable by anything that could not fly.

At the far end there were thirteen steps of pearl that lead up to a golden throne adorned with elaborate carvings and jewels in its frame. The seat and back had silk covered pillows that surely made this throne magnificent. On the throne sat the most decorated elves ever, the ruler of close to half of Xahmore`, the conqueror of any empire that defied his will, unifier of all elves—Telaris Emolian. He watched eagerly as the wizard approached.

"My lord, the time is upon us!" the intruder spoke as he kneeled before Telaris.

"Praylonese, what time do you speak of, and is there any word of Blenadrene returning?" asked the emperor.

"No, my lord, no word yet, and I speak of the time of the Withering. I have seen the black-eyed blotted elf. He destroyed a patrolling fleet as he entered Emolian waters. Surely he has come to start the Withering of Xahmore`!" Praylonese said.

"Why was I not told of his approach, the Withering, so soon?" Telaris Emolian asked.

"We did not know, my lord, but now we must act swiftly against this vile elf, send out the elite guard." Praylonese advised.

"I will not let this vile elf destroy what has been made. I will send out the elite guard!" said the emperor.

"Send three with the order to execute, my lord!" Praylonese advised.

"I will send three of my mightiest guard with orders to execute!" Telaris all but repeated.

"Do you wish me to send down the order, my lord?" Praylonese suggested.

"Yes, Praylonese, send word to the guard on my behalf, I want the black-eyed blotted elf dealt with!" Telaris sat and looked confused and worried.

"Yes, my lord!" the red wizard said with a sly grin.

Praylonese left the throne chamber and entered into the outer hallways. As he reached the room of the guard, he was met by a demon named Nulunar who appeared in the form of an all white elf with grey hair and snake eyes.

"The master is not pleased." said Nulunar. "Telaris was not to know of the black-eyed elf."

"He is still under the spell of Questra, he knows nothing unless we tell him, and cannot think past what we have told him."

"That spell is old, wizard, and cannot be duplicated. Telaris is strong, do not underestimate him or be overconfident in the spell." said the demon.

"There will be no consequence. The elf will be slain soon." Praylonese said confidently.

"By three elite guards," he snickered then said, "You know not of the power with which you deal with, wizard." Nulunar said.

"I knew the master would send you to show his displeasure, and I know you would like to have a chance at killing the elf yourself. So I never planned on sending three guards, I planned on sending three decoys and his assassin. Are you up for the challenge, demon?" Praylonese asked.

Nulunar smiled.

27

WEARY LEGS STRONG HEART

After Rimleon gathered his things from his small wooden home near the docks, he met back with I.

"The journey to the palace will be about a week on horseback, my lord, three on foot," said the old blotted elf to I. "We will have to walk through damned woods and hike treacherous mountains!"

"You are in no condition to make such a journey." Dinora said to the old elf.

"All that I have endured; war, captivity, and torture; was because he is destined to be here. Nothing will keep me from this. This pansy of a walk to the throne." Rimleon said with respectful aggression. He then walked in the direction of the emperor's palace. "Come, destiny is but a few steps in this direction."

The four that could be seen began their walk westward off the docks of Emolia.

The streets were flooded with onlookers pointing and cheering, there were those who were pointing and whispering, those who just looked on and said nothing, and other races who shouted unpleasant words at the travelers.

They said nothing and kept walking.

28

THE UNHOLY PLACE

The docks turned into villages and the villages turned to woods. The old elf led the quest along paths that were thousands of years old. There were plant and animal life, like those neither of the young elves or pixie had ever seen before. They fed on rations Rimleon brought from his home and vegetation from their surroundings. During one of their nights camped in the woods, I decided he would learn a little more about his race's plight and moved his sleeping arrangement next to Rimleon's.

"You said you endured so much because of me and my destiny. Tell me who you are and what you have seen." I said.

"Young one, countless thousands were enslaved and forced to breed in order to own you. Other countless numbers were hunted and killed to keep you from coming." the old elf said.

I said nothing, he just looked at Rimleon in disbelief for a few moments. He looked away and turned back to the old elf with an angered look on his face.

"What about you? What happened to you?" the young blotted, black-eyed elf asked.

"I was a soldier in the army of Telaris Emolian when I was just a boy, easily older than you but younger than most. I fought in countless battles to thwart attempts to harvest blotted elves from Emolia.

"One half of Emolia's coastline was gained in that time in combat to secure the borders so that no one could send an armada from the sea to take the blotted elf in mass numbers.

"My service in the army for over two hundred years earned me various ranks, and I wound up being a warlord that controlled twenty battalions of the most barbaric warriors Xahmore` had ever seen.

"Elfin kind not just the blotted elf was being tested, and we rose to meet the challenge.

"About twenty years into my service as warlord, my soldiers and I ran into the worst possible allied force. Gorlam, King of the trolls, and Dullo, high priest of the human order, joined their armies to round up as many blotted elves as they could. We met them on the plains of Jurojuro. The battle was one of the bloodiest in all the races involved histories. As the battle waged, the humans sent hunters into Emolia. They burned villages and kidnapped what blotted elves they could, mostly children. We won the battle considering the force that they brought in could have destroyed an entire civilization. We held them at bay and the majority of my soldiers were killed, and the blotted ones taken. I was overtaken by Gorlam and Dullo themselves and enslaved in The Unholy Place." Rimleon explained.

"The Unholy Place?" I asked.

"It was what we, who were damned to be there, called it. They had huts packed with females and they only let the strongest of us males live, thinking that the most powerful elf would be spawned from the most powerful they could capture.

Elves born without the black eyes and no significant trace of power were murdered at birth. Our women were also raped, and our highest ranking tortured for secrets of the elfin empire." Rimleon said.

"Why did you not try and escape?" the black-eyed elf continued to inquire.

"When they first brought me in, I was on the edge of death. I was nursed back to health in about a month by the females assigned to me. There were ten women that ranged in age from 25 to 410. I protected, cherished, and loved them all for I was all they had.

"The first time I exited my hut, I saw my people being beaten, humiliated, slain, and raped by the guards and overseers. I tried to stop them, but there were too many powerful beings." Rimleon said with tears in his eyes and pain in his voice. "We were too powerful to just have anyone watching us. They had the most powerful beings in their commands ruling over us. They kept us separated enough, so that we could not unify and overtake them.

"After about 150 years when the fourth cycle of human and troll guards where aged, I overpowered a guard and had him take me, the females, and the children we had to the gate to discover we were thousands of feet above the sea on a rock suspended in mid air, there was no escape. So right at that moment, we waged war on The Unholy Place. We fought with ferocity and the heart of gladiators. Word reached the other parts of the camp and all of the blotted warred with us. For the first and last time we were together.

After most of us fell, they tried to corral us to the center of the rock. No doubt they would just split us up again and start over what they had been doing for close to three hundred years. I could not take it, so I conjured the most powerful soul spear I could and the remaining two hundred or so who had power did whatever we could, and we destroyed the Unholy Place not concerned with our lives but with yours and that you would not exist in that evil place." Rimleon remembered aloud with tears in his eye.

"How did you survive the fall?" the young elf asked.

"I guess the creator saw fit to spare me to live and see this day, but I never thought in the last 230 years I would see you and less even that I would be in your company." the old warlord said.

"I am here now friend, and your suffering and sacrifices have not been in vain." I proclaimed.

I and Rimleon came to know a lot about one another throughout the journey. I was able to learn history and techniques of battle from Rimleon and in turn made Rimleon's life worth living again. The journey was peaceful and full of stories of the past as told by Rimleon. They met no conflict until the second week of the journey when they reached a clearing on the far side of the Mandlius Woods.

29

THE FIELD OF PURPLE

The field on the eastern side of the Mandlius woods was a beautiful field filled with beautiful purple flowers mixed in with high grass. The sun had just begun to set on the western hill, so the sky was a bright orange that blended to a dark blue behind the travelers.

On a hill to the east stood four magnificent horses mounted by four riders, all of whom were dressed for battle in crimson colored armor. I looked to Rimleon.

"Who might this be?" he asked.

"The elite guard," Rimleon answered. "The emperor's most deadly soldiers."

"There is only four of them." said Mlar.

"There is usually just one, my small friend, either the emperor has sent us an escort so that no one is harmed, or you all must be considered a threat of vast consequence." said Rimleon.

"We mean no harm here." I stepped forward and spoke. "We come in peace, we wish an audience with the Emperor."

The elite guard said nothing. The sun sank further behind the hill.

"Let us pass, and we will go in peace as we have come." said I.

"Young elf," said Rimleon, "they are only sent for battle, no words but the emperor's orders are heard by them. Draw your weapon or turn back."

The sun grew closer to the hill and the sky was mostly dark.

One of the knights drew a broadsword that illuminated white when unsheathed. It lit the field and blinded the travelers. I stumbled as he covered his eyes in pain. He unsheathed his blades and listened as one horse charged.

"Lay down in the brush, so they cannot see you." Yelled I.

The horse charged and the young elf listened as the warrior got closer and closer. The hooves pounded the ground like thunder as the clanging from the armor of the warrior shifted giving I perfect inclination of the size and distance away the warrior was from him. Knowing that his state of blindness would not allow him to strike as he would like with his blades, I re-sheathed the blade in his right hand and focused to hear his attacker. The hooves pounded louder and louder, the armor clanged, and I could almost hear a melody between the two.

The hooves now vibrated on the ground where I stood upon. He could hear the stallion breathing with each powerful stride. When he was able to learn the interval in which the armor separated and clanged back together, I envisioned where the guard's helmet met his breast plate as he pulled one of the silver stakes from his waist and threw it in the direction of the rider. The object whistled in the air towards its destination.

The hooves' pounding seemed to shake the entire clearing. As the knight's body went up from the natural progression and his armor left the slightest of openings, the silver stake arrived piercing the knight's throat. The knight fell to the ground dead, and the stallion stopped and stood as majestic as ever. The bright sword began to flicker and then went dark.

"I!" yelled Dinora.

"I am here mother. Stay low in the grass." he said.

I's vision cleared in enough time to see the second rider charge from the hill with a massive shield and unusually long spear-like weapon that extended way beyond the face of the stallion he rode. The rider's charge was swift and smooth.

I jumped upon the steed of the first knight and began to charge the next attacker.

They locked eyes and neither showed fear nor broke stride. I stood upon the back of the stallion and drew both blades. The knight's gaze through his armor became sinister, I's look became focused. As the wind rushed through his locks and the steed moved powerfully under his feet, I became poised.

The two were but seconds from the middle of the clearing closing in on one another. When they finally met, the actions that took place where swift but seemed to take forever. The knight thrust forth his weapon in stride with his fierce charge, and I quickly stepped up onto the spear just over the blade and sprinted down the long handle to reach the guard. As I swooshed by the stallion's head, the knight held up his shield. I swung both swords right to left in stride with his focused charge. The sword in his left hand struck the shield and caused a bright flame as it split the shield in half, from top to bottom and severing the elbow from the joint of the guard. The black diamond blade he swung in his right hand hit the eye slots in the knight's armor and engulfed the rider's head in flames. I continued to run to the back of the long spear-like weapon. Stepping back onto the stallion, he rode to the middle of the clearing.

The body of the second guard fell from the horse with both the severed arm and head on fire in separate areas. I pulled the reigns of the horse to slow him to a complete stop. He then looked to the last two elite guards.

"We do not have to continue this way, I beg you to let us pass." said I with tears welling in his eyes.

No words were spoken.

The third of the elite knights galloped away from the fourth leaving ample distance between the two. The third knight had no weapon. He stretched his hands out to his side and brought them together in front of him in a thunderous clap, blowing I from the horse to the ground. I rolled back onto his feet to see the knight clapping his hands together again as the fourth knight watched. This clap made I feel as if two huge rocks had smashed his body in between them. The knight lifted his clasped hands and I's body lifted into the air as well in a paralyzed state. The knight thrust his hands down and I crashed violently into the ground causing dust to cloud the atmosphere in the clearing. The knight clasped his hands again, lifted I, and then slammed the young elf into a huge tree and knocked it over. The knight did this again and again clapping and slamming I to the ground into trees and on top of rocks, not giving him a chance to react.

There then was a faint whisper in the air.

"Buck," said the soft voice.

The knight's horse then threw him from its back, and he landed with a great thud. This gave I the time he needed to regain his focus. As the guard stood to his feet, he saw the young elf standing but a few feet from him with his swords drawn, with tears in his angry eyes, and his body bloodied and worn. He pointed one sword at the guard and rubbed the blade from the other over the first and a flame spewed from the blades as if a dragon spit it. The flame rushed up the hill and I was right behind it. The flame passed over the spot where the warrior stood and he yelled out in pain. The flame dispelled and left no trace but the magic gauntlets he wore. I reached the top of the hill and looked towards the last guard.

30

THE BLOOD'S KEY

I looked upon the final elite guard with tears streaming down his face. "Let us pass or you will meet the same fate as the others. I do not wish to harm you."

The guard laughed fiendishly.

"Why do you laugh, do you not see your comrades gone on before you?" I said with harshness.

"Child, they were no comrades of mine, no more than they were comrades of yours. They were merely sent so that I could measure your powers and know what must be done to defeat you." The guard said.

The knight removed his helmet to reveal his face.

I looked upon a white elf with white hair and eyes that were like a snakes.

The white elf's armor began to detach from his body and floated in mid-air, revealing his entire body that had no mortal organs. His fingers were long and so were his fingernails. He smiled and showed jagged teeth.

"Demon!" said I.

"My name is Nulunar, now you will know who to name when the creator asks who sent you!" the demon said as he motioned his hands forward.

All the armor floated in the air then flew at I. He was able to dodge most and what he could not dodge he deflected with his swords. When he deflected the last piece, he pointed one sword at the demon and raked the other sword spewing the flame. The demon walked through the flame and was upon him with left hand upon I's throat lifting him from upon the ground. Smiling showing his sharp shark-like teeth Nulunar spoke.

"Silly youngling, I was born from flame, your swords will not give you any added advantage this day."

"Then I will have to destroy you in more barbaric means, demon!" I said.

I dropped his swords grabbed the demon's forearm with his left hand and forced the palm of his right hand into Nulunar's elbow breaking it.

"Aaagggh!" Nulunar shrieked in pain.

I picked up his swords sheathed them and took the fighting stance of the Koawakee, a tribe of humans who fought demons bare handed as a ritual to the creator of all.

The demon's shriek turned into laughter.

"Ha ha ha ha ha ha!" Nulunar laughed as he snapped his arm back in to the socket. "I see, one of the masters of the Koawakee taught you to fight. By the strong base and elevation of your left elbow, I would say Mushaku. I collected his head a few years back."

"Well then, I shall honor his slaying by returning the favor demon." I said vengefully.

They both charged.

The fighting style of the Koawakee was about précise powerful blows to bring excruciating pain. First, you must make the demon show his true form from the pain then remove its head by any means.

Right as the two reached each other, I planted both of his feet into the ground sliding himself ankle deep into the earth leaving two semi-ditches behind him and the first blow I threw was to the chest of Nulunar causing the beautiful face he had to frown in pain as he took a knee.

"Show me who you really are, demon!" I demanded.

Nulunar looked up at I and spit in his direction. He stood and charged I again. I stepped to the side and hit Nulunar in the side of his arm with a powerful chop that smashed it. Nulunar frowned even more as he grabbed his arm.

"Show me who you really are, demon!" I demanded as he chopped Nulunar in the esophagus causing the demon's tongue to come out of his mouth and split in two at the very front like a snake's.

Nulunar fell to his knees grasping his throat. I walked behind the demon as he gasps for air through his crushed airway.

"You will reveal yourself to me now, demon!" I yelled.

I then lifted Nulunar into the air over his head and slammed him over his knee breaking the demon's back.

"Aaaaghh!" Nulunar shrieked out in pain.

I dropped the broken demon on the ground and watched as Nulunar's shape began to shift. Bones popped and his skin boiled as Nulunar screamed in pain and rolled around frantically on the ground. Large, torn bat-like wings sprouted from the demon's back, his sharp teeth became the majority of his face, his skin turned to a dark dirty grey and his eyes grew larger. His knees bent backwards and his feet became as those of a vulture. The demon stood and turned to face I with his true form.

"Now you will die, elf!!" the demon said.

Nulunar charged I and subdued him with overwhelming power. The demon then flapped his massive wings once and took to a tremendous height in the sky. He then bit into

I's neck causing the young elf to scream in agony. Nulunar then let go of the black-eyed elf and I fell from high in the sky limp to the ground. The demon then fell from the sky to the ground and began kicking and gagging in agony. He said only one thing over and over again as he writhed in pain. "Au'braca, Au'braca, Au'braca."

A few minutes later I regained consciousness and crawled to where the demon lay dying.

"It is you who will die this day, demon." I then stood and unsheathed his sword.

Looking down on Nulunar, he saw that the demon's mouth was black with his blood. He raised his sword to strike the last blow and Nulunar spoke.

"Boy, you do not know who you are. Your blood is of Au'braca!" the demon said frantically.

And before Nulunar could consume another breath, I brought down his sword and beheaded the demon. I reached down and lifted the head toward his comrades and then fell down to his knees then to his face, remaining conscious long enough to hear his mother start casting a healing spell as they reached him.

31

A SCENT'S INVITATION

"Is he dead?" asked Mlar reluctantly.

"I doubt it. He took a beating but held his own. I think he just passed out." said Rimleon.

"He will be fine. He would not give up so that he could protect us, and now that the danger has passed he can rest." Dinora said with tears in her eyes.

"We need to gather up all these weapons and armor quickly before the scavenger beasts get a good scent of the death that is here. We would be most unlucky to be here if a Granook or a pack of blooders comes." said Rimleon.

"Granook? Blooders? What are those?" asked Mlar.

"Something that would consider you but an appetizer, little one. Dinora be sure to grab the magical items. Mlar befriend the horses they are some of the best steeds we can ever find. Move quickly. Dinora, I'll put him on a horse. You grab those weapons, they may come in handy." Commanded Rimleon

The three rounded up all that they could. Dinora took the Sword of Light, gave the gauntlets of Braleel to Rimleon, and cast a shrinking spell on Laul's joist and gave it to Mlar.

The four stallions that were left were magnificent, one black, one white, one sorrel, and one blue. Mlar quickly befriended them all and they loaded the gear on the sorrel and blue, and prepped the black and white to ride. Rimleon pulled I off the ground with one hand and draped him in front of his mother on the black steed. He then mounted the white with Mlar.

As soon as the travelers started on their way, Rimleon was alerted by a multitude of birds flying from the trees and all types of animals leaving the woods behind them abruptly.

"Oh no, blooders...Ride! Ride fast! Ride now!" he yelled.

"Yah, yah, yah!" Dinora screamed as she slapped the great steed.

The riders sped away from the woods just before it was overrun by a pack of about thirty blooders. A large, red, dog-like creature that may seem harmless until it smells blood then it goes into an insane state that causes it to try and devour everything in sight. The smell of the dead guard's blood must have made it to them. And now the riders were riding for their lives.

The blooders hopped on the bodies of the fallen guards and were done in what seemed like seconds. One saw the end of the last steed go over the hill and gave chase, the rest of the pack followed.

Rimleon gazed back at the hill with fear in his eyes.

"Hopefully they did not spot us." He said.

"Your hope is misplaced, elf, look!" shouted Mlar.

Rimleon turned back to see the first blooder come over the hill, spotted them out, and broke into a frantic run behind them followed by fifteen or so more.

"By Jyraum'!" said Rimleon. "Ride! Ride you steed or we will all become dinner tonight!"

The horses rode fast and swift into the next thicket of woods. Trees went by as blur, fallen branches and bushes where cleared with ease, but the blooders were closing the gap. The first one reached the last horse that carried the armor and was kicked in the face, busting it wide open and having him devoured by his own pack. The next two came up on the side of the horse and nipped at him from the side while the next one jumped on his back and bit into his neck taking the great steed down. The pack was on it ripping him apart. This gave the riders a little cushion.

"Yah, Yah!" screamed Dinora.

The woods became thicker slowing the stallions pace allowing the blooders to close the gap. The riders could hear the barking and heavy panting getting closer. Dinora cast a pitch black spell that darkened the woods behind them. As the blooders reached the dark, some ran full speed into trees, some jumped each other, but the rest kept coming, the count was about twenty.

As one would get close, Rimleon would toss a soul spear or Mlar an arrow, but the savage pack still pursued. They closed the gap and where coming up on the sides of the riders nipping at the steeds legs. And right as the bush seemed to get its thickest the stallions all jumped into a clearing that had hundreds of huge cattle grazing.

"Yes!" shouted Mlar "The creator must love us!"

"Keep riding, don't look back!" shouted Rimleon.

The blooders hit the clearing and caused a stampede, most of the blooders were trampled but those that were not, killed as many of the cattle as they could while Dinora and the others road off into the next wood blessed to be alive.

32

Secret in the Woods

The riders traveled the majority of the night only stopping before sunrise at a stream to water the horses. They crossed the stream and the horses became spooked, and it took Mlar a while to calm them down.

"Whoa, calm down, it is alright." Spoke Mlar softly.

After the horses were calm, the air was filled with the foulest of aromas.

"Crayton's arse!" swore Mlar, "What is that gravely smell?"

"I don't know, but it is gravely indeed" said Dinora.

"It is the smell of old death, very old." said Rimleon. "Let us continue on our way."

They did and the smell worsened.

When the sun crept over the horizon and through the woods, the smell dissipated as if it were never there.

"The smell, it is gone." said Dinora with a confused tone.

"Who gives a troll rat's backside. I am glad it is gone. I could barely take it, it reminded me of my uncle's gas after rampash stew, oh the agony." said Mlar as he pretended to faint and fall off of Rimleon's shoulder.

"It is rather strange, Dinora. We should not be naive to the scent of death that runs from the sun. Keep your wits about you, pixie!" said Rimleon to Mlar.

They rode with caution making sure that every noise warranted at least a glance in that direction. Among the twigs snapping and the occasional leaves being ruffled by small rodents, there was a faint crying in the distance.

"Do you hear that?" ask Dinora.

"What?" asked Rimleon.

"It sounds as if a child is crying there in the wood."

"We should keep riding. It could be a little monster crying and its mother monster is looking for it right now. What child is in this thick wood this time of morning—" said Mlar as Rimleon interrupted.

"Mlar!"

"And is not dead"

"Mlar!"

"or being eaten by a Jungor—"

"Mlar, silence!" demanded Rimleon.

"Okay, but I am scared. Let's not go that way off the path, into the deep woods." Mlar said quickly.

"What is there to fear, Mlar?" asked Rimleon.

"Uh you mean like the wizard that pulled a boat out of the water and threw fire balls at us, mystical soldiers that were sent to assassinate us, a demon that has the protector and my friend near dead, or the blood thirsty dogs that just chased us? Oh why would I be scared? We aren't having the most peaceful of days! Plus, did I mention the chosen elf that is to be the most powerful of all warriors is out cold on a horse." Mlar said sarcastically.

The two bantered back and forth as Dinora dismounted her steed and walked into the wood following the sounds of the weeping child. Mlar looked to her horse and saw that she was gone.

"Look now, she is gone into the woods like there is nothing that eats flesh out there!" said Mlar.

"Shut your face, child!" said Rimleon.

"It's a monster." Mlar said as he made an ugly face and positioned his hands like claws and leaned at Rimleon as if to attack him.

Dinora meanwhile found the source of the tears. It was a male human child with a laceration on his leg.

"Are you okay? How did your leg begin to bleed?" asked Dinora.

"I was running and when the sun came through the trees, I was blinded momentarily and fell over that rock." The child said in a whimper.

"Can you walk?" Dinora asked.

"No." the child said softly.

"Come, I will carry you." Dinora said.

She picked up the small child and walked back towards her guild. She reached them and to their surprise she was carrying a human child.

"Here she comes, Mlar. What is she carrying?" asked Rimleon.

"It looks like a baby monster with blood on it, we are doomed!!" Mlar replied.

"You fool, it is a child." Rimleon said.

Rimleon got off his horse and took the child from Dinora and placed him on the pack horse and walked back to Dinora.

"Why did you save that human child?" Rimleon asked in disgust.

"Where I come from all races got along, and this child has done nothing and he should not be judged by his predecessors' actions." Dinora answered in a condescending tone.

Dinora walked back to the pack horse.

"Child, where do you live?" she asked.

"That way." The child said as he pointed.

"We will take you home. We could use a little rest ourselves!" said Dinora with a smile.

She looked at Rimleon sternly and walked past him to her steed and son. She mounted the horse and patted its backside to start its trot. Rimleon looked at Mlar and Mlar repeated his ugly face and claw lean towards him. Rimleon mounted his steed and followed behind Dinora to the child's home. After a short ride through the wood, the riders came upon an overcrowded village and were greeted by smiling faces of all races. It appeared that they were now in a better situation.

33

SPELL OF DISSIPATION

"You block a spell by forcing blood to the hand and placing your hand on the spell's path." Spoke a familiar voice to I.

I awoke slowly and spoke, "Lomerian? Where am I? Am I dead?" asked I.

The young elf looked around and was in what appeared to be a great hall. It was empty with a high ceiling, double pillars from one unseen end to the other, and was a milky marble. The air was cold and dry. I looked across the room and saw the great wizard moving his hands as to draw a picture in the air then moved them towards I. A flame jumped from Lomerian's hand towards the young elf.

"Defend yourself or face excruciating pain!" said the great wizard.

The flame reached the elf and he leaped to avoid it. The flame followed.

"You block a spell by forcing blood to the hand and then placing your hand in the spell's path!" the great wizard said again.

I began to descend and the flame continued its rise toward him. So he began to dive at the flame with both hands in front of him, flexing every muscle from his elbow to his fingers to ensure blood would be in his hand. When he met the huge flame, there was a loud boom and the flame burst into sparks of bright orange light that fizzled out as they touched the ground.

"More training, Lomerian?" I asked as a bored child.

"If you plan to retrieve Blenadrene, you will need to know how to combat magic." Lomerian scolded.

"Where is he?" asked I.

"An old witch will guide you to him, she will want the Sword of Light the elite guard had in return for the information. You must not let her have it. The sword holds greater power than anyone who has held it ever knew, but her. Now sit here." said the great wizard.

Lomerian pointed to the spot at his feet. I walked to the spot and sat one leg crossed over the other. Lomerian sat across from I and touched the blotted elf's forehead.

"The power of magic lies in the soul, the focus to harness and manipulate it comes from the mind. Faith and focus, emotions and attitude determine the power of a spell," said the great wizard. "Follow my lead."

Lomerian began to touch both his thumbs with one finger at a time on the respective hand. Every time he pulled a finger back, there was a small line of energy that connected his fingers to his thumb.

I was attentive.

"This is what is used to cast a spell, it is your life force coupled with the energy in the atmosphere that surrounds you." Lomerian explained.

Lomerian then began to move his fingers to draw in the air with the energy then touched what he drew with his right hand and a great bird of lightning formed and flew around the vast room crackling from one spot to another.

Lomerian then drew another spell, reached out, and grabbed it to create a spear of green energy. He held the spear up as if he was about to throw it and just released his grasp. I watched as the spear tore through the air and destroyed the bird of lightning with a great explosion then implosion into nothing.

"Now, you try." said Lomerian.

"I do not know any spells, Lomerian." the young elf said.

"Young one, the greatest of spell casters created spells. They did not need scrolls. They wrote them! The feeling and imagination combined with a great magic on the inside brings forth brilliant magic on the outside!" Lomerian declared.

"I understand, master." I said.

I then closed his eyes to clear his thoughts and felt his emotions and surroundings. His eyes opened abruptly, and he closed both of his hands into a fist and opened them to reveal one bright white and one black sphere of energy. With his right hand he waved over the air and the black sphere wrote out on the air in ancient word, Lomerian read it and was almost horrified. I touched it and the writing turned to black flames that danced around the room. He did the same with the white sphere and the flames danced around the room growing larger and heating the atmosphere.

Lomerian looked disturbed but stood firm with a hand close to his eyes to block the light that danced the room. Then the young elf brought his hands together and the flames touched, condensing into a small sphere. Lomerian hurried and drew a blue sphere of his own and held it tight in his hands before the small sphere exploded without a sound and rippled the air, warmed the room, and did no harm to anything.

"Lomerian, it is time they have reached the dead village." said Rune.

"Very well, young one, remember that spell when you are in danger of loosing your life to magic. Those words were of a tongue that can't be spoken by us, and that kind of spell will humble an unwise spell caster." the elder elf said.

Lomerian then cracked open the sphere he had and chilled the air again.

"It is time for you to rejoin your guild"

Lomerian cast a spell, touched I's shoulder, and I passed out on the floor and began to fade away.

"He will be tough to beat, Lomerian." said Tleisha.

"I know but it was necessary to train him this hard. How else would any of this have been possible?" said Lomerian.

"What now?" asked Tleisha.

"Has the Orc left?" asked Lomerian.

"Yes, he will be born soon." Rune answered.

"The creator blessed him with the Orc in the midst of all this. Now we must leave him before we are discovered. We can find our way from here." suggested Lomerian.

34

Village of the Witch

I awoke in a bed made mostly of straw, inside of a hut that was red clay and rock. The roof were long boards holding up straw and twig. There was a counter with fresh bread and fruit sitting on it. The doorway was small and had a thick piece of cloth separating the room from the hall. As Dinora noticed he was awake, she stroked his locks and spoke.

"Welcome back, son, you had me worried. The demon had bitten you to deep." she said as a worried mother.

"I am well, mother, do not fret. The demon did not do much damage." he said as a male child.

He reached for his wound and discovered it was gone, and he felt revitalized.

"How long have I been asleep?" I inquired.

"You were unconscious almost a full day, my son." Dinora replied.

"Thank you for helping me heal, mother, where are we?" He asked as he looked around.

"We stumbled into a small village just a few days east of the palace." She answered.

"Who is the keeper of this village?" he asked.

"I am." Said a beautiful female elf who walked into the hut to the back of I holding a bowl of stew. "I am Eauta. You all got here this morning and you looked pretty bad but now you seem to be healed fine."

I turned and looked at the fair elf, and she saw his eyes and dropped the bowl and looked frightened.

"What is the matter?" asked Dinora.

"It is him. The black eyed blotted elf, the slayer of the beast. The prophecy is true!" Eauta said.

The girl elf ran from the small hut.

"Have you seen anyone else, mother?" I asked.

"Yes, there are many elves, orcs, and a few humans in this small village. I don't see where they all can sleep though it is not that big a place." Dinora said.

"They don't, this is a dead village, mother, and its keeper is an old, powerful witch."

"How do you know, son?"

"A spirit told me while I slept."

"Then we must leave at once!" Dinora said.

"No, she knows where Blenadrene is, and I won't leave until I know as well." I said, "Where are the others?"

"Rimleon and Mlar are outside tending to the horses we gained from the battle with the guard." Dinora answered. "She knows where Blenadrene is? How? Who is this witch?"

"I am not sure. Did we gather the weaponry from the guards as well as the horses?" I asked.

"Yes, Rimleon insisted, but we lost the armor."

"Where is the Sword of Light?" I inquired.

"I have it." Dinora showed I.

"Good, mother, keep it close to you and you to me. The witch will want it, but we must not let her have it. The power it has is known only by a few, and she is one of those who knows." I explained.

"How would a lowly old witch know of a power that is so secret and not he who wielded the sword in battle?" Dinora asked.

"Maybe she is not so lowly of a witch." I deduced, "How many would you say are in this village, from what you saw earlier?"

"A few hundred or so, son. Why?"

"Could a lowly witch with a cauldron and a few snake heads claim so many, mother? Let us take a walk and check on our friends."

I threw back the cloth draped over the front of the mud and grass hut expecting to see the many inhabitants, but saw no one. He looked to the right and saw the horses they rode tied to a tree, but no signs of his friends.

"Be ready, mother." I said softly as he drew his swords.

"There will be no need for those, young hero." said a woman's voice.

I and Dinora looked to the far end of the village and there stood the beautiful elfin girl who was the keeper of the village draped in a blue robe of the Yorenzana. She waved her hand and pulled a nearby table and chairs in front of her.

"Come, sit, and let us talk." She suggested.

"Where are my friends?" asked I.

"They are safe, not in harm's way at all. I just needed it to be us right now. It is not everyday you cross paths with legends. Rimleon the great general and destroyer of The Unholy Place, and the chosen slayer of the beast, come sit."

I sheathed his blades and he and Dinora sat with the female elf.

"Tell me, young elf, what brings you to my village?"

"Destiny has a way of putting you where you must be at any appointed time." I replied.

"What part do I play in this destiny you speak of? Your destiny is with the beast."

"One must walk different paths and overcome trials in order to complete destiny, if none of this were necessary, life would have no meaning, no story. The beginning and the end would touch and not have the space to be their own entity." the young elf replied.

"I am no obstacle for you, I do not wish to impede your progress, nor do I want to test your power. So tell me, young one, why has destiny led you to me? I am sure your guides have told you." the witch inquired.

"You know where a friend of ours is. And we would like to have him back with us." Dinora said.

"What friend do you speak of?" Eauta asked.

"Blenadrene." I stated.

"Blenadrene?" Eauta said, surprised, "Oh my, if you think I know where he is, that means that he has finally been captured. Hmm…So that is who the Washta is for. What wizard was powerful enough to capture Blenadrene, the Lord of War?"

"Praylonese took Blenadrene." I said.

"Surely you jest, he is no match for Blenadrene. Either he wanted to be captured or he was not himself. Praylonese is powerful, but Blenadrene is power." Eauta proclaimed.

"Whatever the situation was, he was taken. Do you know where he is?" interjected Dinora.

The witch paid her no mind and just stared at I.

"What is this Washta you speak of?" asked I.

The witch then stared at Dinora.

"What is the Washta?" asked I once more.

The witch looked back at I.

"It is a ceremony in which a great magic is destroyed. This one is sure to be the most powerful in centuries." answered Eauta.

"Do you know where he is?" asked I.

"I may, but do you have anything that I may want in return for the question?" Eauta said.

The elf stretched forth her hand and waved it in front of the son and mother, and paused at Dinora. She drew her hand back looked away with her fist clenched, then looked back with a slight touch of disgust in her eyes.

"I will help you. Come with me if you wish to see Blenadrene alive." the witch said.

Eauta stood then turned her back to the son and mother, She began to rotate her right hand in spiral from large to small. Everything in front of her began to ripple like a puddle, a small stone fell in.

"Come quickly before they feel the tare!" Eauta said as she stepped into the rippling reality.

I and Dinora followed with no concern for themselves but for the one who protected and loved them for so long.

35

Punishment of Pain

Inside the dark stone chamber, the deep voice spoke.

"You have disappointed me, Praylonese. Not only have you disobeyed me, but you have put my plans in jeopardy."

"Master, I only wanted to destroy the elf to please you."

"Fool, you cannot put yourself into destiny to claim greatness. Destiny creates the time for beings to become great! One of my most powerful minions is lost and yet you stand before me untouched! I cannot allow that to be so. You must be punished." The voice in the darkness said.

"Master, please allow me another chance!" begged Praylonese.

The figure raised one finger from its resting place on the stone throne which he sat upon. Praylonese looked in fear as his master lowered the lone finger that sent a green line that cracked across the red wizard's face as a whip splitting it to the bone. Praylonese screamed out in great agony.

"You will be given one more chance, wizard. If you fail, you will not die by my hands. Find where Blenadrene has placed the knowledge of the shard before they free him." The voice in the darkness commanded.

"Who can reach him?" Praylonese asked exhaustedly from his hands and knees with blood dripping from his face.

"I cannot tell, but they approach from the west of him. There where three but now only two. Go!" demanded the voice in the dark.

The red wizard pulled himself from the floor and backed out of the room chanting a healing spell upon his wound.

36

THE HIGH WIZARD

As they stepped through the ripple, the three elves were in the middle of a blizzard that made it hard for them to see each other. The air was cold and dry, and the wind howled like a pack of wolves serenading the heavens.

"What kind of trick is this?" asked Dinora.

"This is no trick. We are in the same realm as your beloved Blenadrene." answered Eauta.

"Where are we exactly?" asked I.

"Nowhere." Eauta answered.

"Well where do we go from here, what do we do?" asked I.

"We do nothing but wait. I put us someplace where the magic is too strong to feel even though you enter this realm, young elf. We will wait." the witch answered.

The three elves waited as the snow continued and the wind howled madly. Hours went by and then a whistle that sounded like a bird's song came from a distance. Eauta then held up her hand, and it illuminated a blue light. The song got closer and closer.

"If I was you, young elf, I'd pull my hood over, so no one could see my face. Besides, those eyes may startle my griffin." Eauta said.

I reached back for the cloak no one could see. He pulled the hood over his head and both his mother and the witch turned and looked his way in amazement.

"I can't feel him anymore, can you?" Eauta asked Dinora.

"No, I cannot. His hood must hide what he is, as well as who he is, and the power he wields." Dinora said as she reached out to touch I.

"This will be easier than I thought then." Eauta said.

Just as Eauta finished her statement, her griffin landed. White as the snow, it towered over the three elves. Eauta lowered her hand and the griffin crouched down.

"Climb on. He will take us to the place they are holding Blenadrene." Eauta said.

The elves climbed on and the griffin flapped his huge wings and lifted into the sky. The strong, magnificent creature navigated the winds with ease.

The snow began to ease up after about a twenty-minute flight to reveal two tall pillars standing alone in a vast field of snow. In between the two pillars floated what appeared to be a mummified body.

"There he is bound and helpless." said Eauta. "We must keep our distance, or they will know we are here."

"How will we help him, if we cannot get close?" asked Dinora.

"I can go. They cannot sense him through his cloak." said Eauta.

"Son, you mu—"

Dinora looked to where I was sitting on the Griffin and he was gone.

"Look on the ground approaching Blenadrene." announced Eauta.

It was I running through the snow. His black cloak covered every move he made, making him look like a phantom gliding across the icy terrain. As I got closer, he noticed the ground around Blenadrene was desert sand and that the temperature was very hot. Right as he reached the outer perimeter of the pillars and sand, a small red light appeared right in front of where the dirt met the snow, then there was a bright flash of red and I stopped to see a figure step out of the red light. When the light faded, there stood Praylonese with his red hair and beard blowing in the snowy wind. He had a fresh scar across his face that resembled half an x.

"Who are you?" scoffed the wizard.

I said nothing.

"How did you get here?"

I said nothing.

"Why are you here? Answer me, before I pull the answer from you?" Praylonese demanded as he lifted his right hand that had red energy crackling around it.

I unsheathed one of his swords, and to the red wizard it just appeared that the cloak flapped hard in the wind, he could see nor hear anything under the cloak but darkness.

"Very well then, intruder, fall!" said the red wizard.

Praylonese pressed his hand forth and the electric energy crackled towards I. I placed his hand forward to block the spell, and it appeared to Praylonese that the lightning was absorbed by darkness.

"Who are you? What are you?" asked the red wizard.

"I have come for the wizard," said I in a faint whisper. "Release him."

"No, he will be bound until the Washta, and he will be destroyed. If you want him, you will have to take him."

"It would be my pleasure." Said the black-eyed blotted elf.

I drew his other sword and raked one blade over the other, sending a more fierce flame than the ones before toward Praylonese.

Praylonese then cast a shielding spell that protected him from the flame but not the force at which it came at him. The flames' pressure knocked the red wizard from his feet into the burning sands. I was on him before he could rise to his feet with a boot on his neck and blade on his forehead.

"I know it is you, boy. The flame that killed Tugarlo looked just like that. Show yourself." demanded Praylonese.

I pulled back his hood and the cloak disappeared.

"You have been beaten, wizard, and with ease!" I said.

"I am not done yet, boy!" Praylonese said as he tried to conjure up a spell to no avail.

"There is no magic here, you are helpless." I said.

"No matter, you still cannot free your beloved Blenadrene." The red wizard said the best he could with a boot on his esophagus.

I showed Praylonese a blue sphere he had stored in his palm before entering into the hot sands. He cracked it open and the air around the sands began to cool and the snow began to fall on the burning sands slowly. Magical energy then rushed into the void and the snow began to swirl around I and Praylonese. I then stepped off of the wizard's neck and sheathed his sword.

"Foolish boy, now I will be able to unleash my darkest magic upon you!"

The wizard charged himself with the surrounding magic causing his eyes to glow and his body to be surrounded with the red crackling energy.

"Try and you will surely perish, red one!" I said.

And right as Praylonese was about to turn his fury on I, a huge green bolt of lightning crashed down on him from above causing him to lie on the ground shaking and burning to a crisp.

I looked to the sky where the mummified body was floating and saw Blenadrene with an infuriated look on his face, green energy crackling around his hand and in his eyes and the cloth used to bind him tattered and torn hanging off him.

"We must leave here, young one. Danger approaches." said Blenadrene as his weak body fell to the ground.

I ran to his side and helped him up.

37

Oldest Deceit

The snow fell heavy as the young elf helped Blenadrene to his feet. His body was scared and his robe torn.

"We must leave at once!" Blenadrene said almost horrified. "How did you get here?"

"An old witch opened a portal here for us."

"Us, what do you mean us?" Blenadrene asked I.

"My mother is here, we can leave here as soon as we find her."

"What? No she must not be here, it is too dangerous, where is she? We must find her and leave at once!!" Blenadrene said frantically.

No sooner than Blenadrene spoke those words the white griffin landed in front of them. Dinora ran to Blenadrene and hugged him. Blenadrene looked at Eauta with extreme displeasure. She smiled at him.

"We must go he is almost here." shouted Blenadrene.

"Yes, I feel a presence too, so powerful it almost hurts." said Eauta.

"Eauta you must take us from here I am still too weak to open this realm." said Blenadrene.

"It may be to late." said Eauta. "Look!"

The four powerful beings all looked off into the snow to see a massive figure that looked to be an ogre or a troll walking towards them. But it was something far more massive and far more powerful. The snow began to blow from all directions towards the figure coming through the snow. And there was a deep, deep evil laugh that came from the shadowy outline in the snow.

"Yorenzana!" said Blenadrene.

"Yorenzana?" asked Dinora with a confused tone.

"Is not Yorenzana a way of magic not a being?" ask Eauta.

"No, I learned at the end of the battle against the Shamual that Yorenzana was a powerful demon, one of the beast's generals. Thousands of years ago he enslaved the elvin throne with a spell and began a conquest of Xahmore`. He started a society of elfin magic and secretly recruited the most blessed with magic and had his disciples teach them more. Only one wizard of the Yorenzana is permitted to see him at a time and when that wizard dies a new one is selected. It is usually the most dark-hearted of us. I do not know who it was during my time. The most powerful of us who he knew could not be corrupted where given orders through the emperor.

Yorenzana's teachings coupled with our almost infinite lifespan enabled us to learn more, making our magic the most powerful. That is how the elves have stayed in power so long, and I helped him until I learned the truth. He wants what I was given on that mountaintop years ago, so he can free his master. That is why I was brought here, but I no longer have It." said Blenadrene as he looked at Dinora.

"That is why I was able to see those things in my dreams, why give it to me?" asked Dinora.

"If I would have given it to I he would not have had the time to become as strong as he is now. They knew not of you and once I returned, I knew they would be after it. But since you are in the magical realm, he must have felt it.

Now he has come for it. Eauta open a portal, we must try to avoid this fight!" Blenadrene yelled to the witch.

The sorceress waved her hand in the spiral motion from large to small and reality rippled in front of them. Dinora and Eauta entered first, and I and Blenadrene backed into it with their eyes on Yorenzana who was still walking their way, laughing in a deep tone. They came through the portal standing in the middle of the dead village. They made it. Dinora ran to Blenadrene and hugged his neck intensely. Eauta stood with a confused look on her face at what she had just seen and heard. I just stared towards where they came through.

"Blenadrene, why did you keep this knowledge to yourself for so long leaving the rest of us blind?" asked Eauta.

"I was ashamed of what I had done, and I was guided by my master to wait on the time of the black-eyed elf to return here. Besides you would not have done anything good with the knowledge, but maybe try and seek out Yorenzana for your own evil purposes."

She just smiled and waved her hand at two small trees in the area and they returned to their true forms of Rimleon and Mlar.

"I still have honor and respect inside of my dark heart, lover." said Eauta.

Mlar flew to I and latched onto his neck in shear delight to see his friend. Rimleon walked up to the witch with a disgusted look on his face.

"Watch yourself, general, you could be a slave for a second term if I so desire." said Eauta with a sly grin.

"One day, witch, you will earn your death." He said as he walked over towards I who had not taken his eyes from where they had come.

Blenadrene turned his attention back to Dinora.

"You must give me back the shard Dinora now that they know you have it they will come for you no matter where you are." said Blenadrene.

"Now that they know of me, would they not come anyway?" she replied.

"They would until they tracked it down." Blenadrene replied as a father.

"Then I will keep it, master. When they come for it, we will be ready!"

I drew both his swords and looked back. "Well, I suggest we all prepare to fight. He is coming for it now, if you haven't noticed it is starting to snow!!"

"Battle ready!" cried Blenadrene.

Everyone took a stance for combat as the sky turned white and in the distance an evil deep underlying laugh could be heard.

38

General of the Beast

Yorenzana watched as the elves walked into the rift between realities. Before the portal could close behind them, he put his hand in the snow in front of him and lifted it causing a wave of snow to rush towards the portal. The wave reached the portal and froze it solid causing the rift to fall flat to the ground. He walked towards it, chanting ancient words in his demon tongue. As he reached the frozen doorway, he looked into it and saw the elves. He then stretched forth both his hands touching his index fingers and thumbs together making a circle. White energy filled the circle and he pulled his hands apart widening the circle until it was the same size as the frozen rift. The circle of energy floated down on top of the rift and Yorenzana lifted his foot high to his chest and stomped down on the rift.

BOOM!

The elves found themselves covered with snow and back in the realm of Yorenzana's magic only a hundred feet or so from the large demon. They gazed upon him in awe. His face was that of a black wolf, his build was of a giant, and he towered over the elves some six times over. This huge demon wore a robe of gold and grey. The gold outlined the robe and the grey that covered him was smoke that made faces of evil and agony as he moved.

"Ahhh Blenadrene, my most powerful pupil, I see you have finally returned with what the emperor asked you for so many years ago." Yorenzana's deep voice bellowed. "I believe you have something I desire to have, elfin girl. Come so I may relieve you of it."

"She will not give you the shard, demon!" said Blenadrene.

"She does not appear to share the same thoughts as you, Blenadrene."

Dinora's eye's where transfixed on Yorenzana as she began to walk towards him slowly.

"Dinora, no!" screamed Blenadrene.

"She cannot hear you. She belongs to me now." Yorenzana said.

"Attack, all of Xahmore` is now in peril, Attack!" commanded Blenadrene.

The assault began with Blenadrene submerging his hands in the snow and charging himself to where every strand of hair was crackling with the green energy, his skin seemed to glow as his eyes did. He then pulled his hands from the snow and they were covered with two spheres of light so bright, the faces on Yorenzana's robe covered their eyes. He brought his hands together and the light shot from him with the force of one hundred cannons in a continuous flow. Right before it reached the demon wizard, a portion of smoke from the robe went to meet the energy blast and began to absorb it.

Rimleon placed his hands inside of the magical gauntlets and conjured his soul spear. The gloves magnified it immensely to a power he had never felt. He hurled it at Yorenzana, and it crackled through the air and the smoke from another part of his robe shot out and met the spear causing an explosion that caused the snow to gust from the space back towards all parties involved.

Eauta threw mental daggers that where swallowed by the robe and thrown back at her. She caused them to dissipate into thin air as they reached her.

"I, grab your mother!" Blenadrene yelled.

I ran up to Dinora and was thrown back by a transparent energy, landing upon his back.

"Your mother is mine now, black-eyed one! My master will be set free soon!" said Yorenzana as he began to laugh again.

Dinora was helpless as she walked toward the demon one slow step in the snow after the other. She could see what was happening around her but could not control her body in any way. She struggled to gain control but her attempts were in vain. She began to cry as she looked towards Yorenzana's wolf-like face smiling at her.

I did all he could to help his mother but was not yet powerful enough to thwart the spell of the demonic wizard. He charged and was blown back by the smoke. He threw spikes, and they were caught by the smoke and thrown back at him. In a blind rage, he raked his swords together to spew a flame at Yorenzana. It was intense, melting all the snow in its path. The smoke darted out to stop the flame but could not as the flame continued to its destination, Yorenzana.

As the flame reached him, Yorenzana grabbed the flame and moved it like a whip and flung back at I. I placed his swords in front of him to block the flame and the swords reclaimed it. Dinora continued her walk getting closer to Yorenzana.

"Why do you fight me? I am the magic that you use. You cannot win!" spoke the demon to his aggressors.

"Concentrate everything you have into his chest, Eauta, do as I do; and, Rimleon, wait for us then you occupy his hands, I follow with the flame." Blenadrene ordered. "Where is Mlar?"

"The coward is probably hiding somewhere!" stated Rimleon.

"He is no coward," said I, "Maybe too cautious sometimes but not a coward!"

"NOW!" screamed Blenadrene.

Eauta submerged her hands into the snow and overcharged herself with the energy of the realm. Her hair began to crackle with a blue energy, and she too shot light to join Blenadrene. The smoke from the robe met the light and absorbed it.

Rimleon then conjured two soul spears and hurled them at the demon, after which, he attempted to clap the gauntlets together to smash Yorizana the same way I had been in the field. The smoke destroyed the spears and before Rimleon could clap the gauntlets together, Yorizana positioned his huge hands to his sides to stifle the magic of the gauntlets. Dinora was almost arm's length away from the demon.

Yorinzana then heard a buzzing sound.

I then spewed the flame from the swords of Jambesha; the smoke failed to stop it again, and it would surely strike the demon this time but two more arms and hands came from under the robe of smoke and grabbed it. Dinora was now at his feet. He began to boast.

"Fools, this is my realm. I am the supreme being here, and you have lost. You cannot even touch me in all of your most powerful efforts."

The buzz then became louder, to the point it was right in Yorenzana's ear, then it stopped. After a second of silence, Yorenzana screamed out in great pain. He grabbed his ear that was full of blood. This allowed Rimleon to touch the gauntlets together smashing the demon, causing him to release I's flame that engulfed the robe of smoke making the faces scream out in agony as the flame destroyed them. That allowed the barrage of light from Blenadrene and Euata to finally touch Yorinzana causing him to be knocked back.

Rimleon began tossing soul spears as fast as he could conjure them. The assault became too much and the demon took his index finger and sliced reality behind him and stepped slowly back into the realm he had come from. His spell on Dinora was broken, and she fell to her knees in exhaustion. The elves did not let up. I continued to spew the flames as he walked closer to his mother to retrieve her. He grabbed her by her shirt and began to pull her away from the wolf-faced demon of magic.

Yorenzana was all the way inside the split in reality looking over the elves and a pixie with a bloodied joist with disgust, and right as the portal was about to close, he smiled the most evil of smiles.

"All of your efforts were admirable, and that is all they were!" Yorenzana said with conviction as he stretched forth his right hand and levitated Dinora to his palm so fast that the force of the pull ripped her from her outer clothes as I tried pulling her to safety.

He then turned to see his mother's partially clothed body in the palm of the demon's hand as the portal closed swiftly.

"Mother!" he screamed at the top of his lungs, "Mother!"

"We have failed." said Rimleon.

"Open a portal, we must follow him!" Proclaimed I.

"We cannot follow him to where he has gone, for it is nowhere." said Blenadrene.

I kneeled in the snow with his mother's clothes in hand and wept into them. Eauta walked over and put her hands on I's shoulder. Blenadrene followed.

"There is no time to weep, I, now is the time to act. He will not take the shard from your mother until he reaches the throne under which his master is sealed, so she will live until then." said Blenadrene.

I then spoke with tears in his eyes and rage in his voice, "Then we must get there first!"

There was an immense flash of light behind the four males that dissipated quickly.

"Where is the witch?" asked I.

"She must have run off." said Rimleon.

I then began to look through his mother's clothes frantically.

"The witch has taken the Sword of Light. Lomerian said not to let her have it." said I.

"We will deal with her treachery another day. Come we must make it to the throne before Yorenzana does." said Blenadrene as he raised his hands to the sky and formed a green void right above his head that he floated into.

Rimleon walked under it next and lifted into it as well. I stood holding his mother's clothes looking into the snow where the demon had taken her.

"I, let's go, time is of the essence." said Mlar.

"I know, but I want to let my anger fester just a while longer so that I will act without remorse for my enemies the next time I face them." I looked out into the snowy realm and yelled, "Hear me, demons, I will come for you all. I will slay you. I will protect all that is good in this world and will not rest until you all are one with your destiny, and witch we will see you again and our meeting will not involve talks and false alliances but your surrender or death!"

He then pulled over his hood and walked toward the green void.

Mlar turned and floated up into the portal.

I then opened his hands to show a white and black sphere. He released them both and as the flames began to dance around in the snow, he too levitated into the green void and it sealed.

39

History in Crystal

The black-eyed, blotted elf rose through the green portal into a city that appeared to be covered in ice. The buildings stood tall and majestic as they shimmered in the midday sun. The streets were slick round stones placed side by side, and they gleamed like diamonds.

I looked past the buildings to the skyline and saw mountains, glorious mountains that looked as if they were painted by the creator just a moment ago. The mountains were covered with colorful vegetation and alive with the most beautiful of creatures. He then thought to himself if these mountains are warm enough to support this type of life, then how is this city of ice able to stand?

He turned to see Blenadrene looking at him with tears in his eyes.

"I never thought this day would be necessary, but now I see that Ulrant was right." said Blenadrene.

"What do you mean?" I asked.

"Follow me, I."

Blenadrene led I and the others through the city of ice.

No sign of life seemed to grace this magnificent place. The silence was ghostly. I could feel a presence but there appeared to be none. They walked through the streets for a great distance before they reached a narrow alley that entered into a clearing that was the courtyard that prefaced an enormous staircase. While in the alley, I could only see a portion of the courtyard and steps past Blenadrene's tall frame.

"Is this the city of the Emolian Palace?" asked I.

"No, young one, this is the place we will find our army. This is where I discovered the truth. This is the city of the Shamual." answered Blenadrene.

"How can this be? Rune told me you and your army destroyed all of this."

"Rune 'the Dwarf Barbarian' told you of this place?" Blenadrene asked I.

"Yes, he was one of the beings that came with Lomerian to train me." I replied.

"There is a lot about that story that was misconstrued, young one. And to hear it from Rune means someone must have been peering in and could not see it all as it unfolded or they have told a great lie." proclaimed Blenadrene.

As they walked out of the alley into the vast courtyard, the three elves and pixie bore witness to thousands of elves and Shamual frozen in the middle of a great battle. The scene was legend suspended in time.

"What majesty!" said Rimleon.

"By the creator!" said Mlar softly.

"Blenadrene, did you do this?" asked I.

"I am powerful, I, but not powerful enough to sustain a spell for a hundred years that I am not in the presence of. No the magic that did this is far greater than mine." he replied.

"Then what happened here? Where is this army you spoke of? Why are we not on our way to the Emolian Palace to save my mother?" I said out of anger and frustration.

"Your mother is not all that is at stake, boy!" Blenadrene replied sternly.

There was a silence in the courtyard as the two stared at each other with conviction. Then I looked away from Blenadrene and took a knee out of respect to his mother's master and his male caregiver.

"You are right, Blenadrene, forgive me. My personal feelings have become too intertwined with the matter at hand."

"No need for apologies. I am at war with my emotions as well. Come, my young protector, all of your questions will be answered."

The warriors in this frozen battle covered the entire courtyard and half of the steps. There where great elfin warriors standing here suspended in battle that legend said had been lost. The race of Shamual that had been rarely seen and not even spoke of in hundreds of years was represented in a number that was hard for the visitors to make out.

The walk continued through the real-life statues of ice towards the stairs. At the bottom of the stairs, the elves where trying to advance to the palace. The Shamual appeared to be trying to thwart the invasion. The further up the stairs they climbed, the fewer warriors appeared to be in battle, but more so elves where dead around one huge Shamual who appeared to be diving to attack something that was not there.

"Is this Muline?" asked I as he stared at the huge cat-like being.

"It is. One of the most powerful, if not the most powerful warrior I ever faced. He is the first one of his kind. A mountain cat augmented by Ulrant to be his protector. " Blenadrene just stared in awe at the presence of the great

Shamual leader. "Now we need him and every one of them that fought in this great battle, for there is one far greater to come."

"How can this be undone?" asked Rimleon. "If you did not have the power to cast the spell then, how will you break it?"

"There is a piece missing to this puzzle that must be returned. Do not interfere." said Blenadrene as he walked around to the front of Muline and began to chant deeply.

He walked over to a space on the stairs that was not frozen and laid there facing the great Muline who was mid-air and looked as if he were about to attack the wizard. Blenadrene's half-naked body became adorned with a green robe that was torn and dirty. His body became wounded and his face bloodied as he stretched out his hand towards the great cat.

Blenadrene's companions looked on in amazement.

And then off in the distance the sounds of swords clashing and roars that shook the soul began to fill the air. They looked to see that the city was being freed from its icy entrapment.

The ice began to evaporate from the horizon towards the crystal palace, but it did not mist away into water but seemed to dissipate into thin air as if it were being unwrapped into a light and gathered into a breeze that floated toward the palace. As the ice lifted from the city, it revealed that the structures were all made of crystal and where the most brilliant of hues glowed in the sunlight. The ice continued to unravel towards the courtyard and when it lifted from the beings in the courtyard, the battle began to wage on as if the hundreds of years had not passed. More roars were heard and more weapons clashed until there was all out mayhem in the courtyard of the Shamual once more.

"Should we help?" asked Mlar to I.

"Blenadrene said that we should not to interfere, there must be a reason. Be patient, little one." said Rimleon before I could respond.

The ice then cleared the courtyard and made its way up the staircase freeing all as it wove away from them. Elves tried to rush up the stairs and Shamual engaged them to stop their attempt. And then in a blink of an eye the spell lifted from Muline and the roar that had been held back for hundreds of years bellowed throughout the mountains as he continued his dive towards Blenadrene in hopes of slaying the high wizard. But Blenadrene's chant was complete and thwarted the dive with a spell that repelled the large Shamual. Muline was sent into a flip towards the bottom of the stairs but was able to gather himself and land on his feet. When he landed, he cracked the crystal steps.

He stood and his stature was awesome and his presence made every one near him take notice and make provisions to move from the path between him and Blenadrene. Standing upright, he roared again even louder than before and charged Blenadrene. From his upright stance he went on all fours and bolted up the stairs.

Blenadrene stood and awaited Muline.

As the humanized mountain cat closed in on Blenadrene, the light over everyone's head floated into the palace. Blenadrene cast spell after spell that Muline dodged on his way up the crystal staircase toward him. Blenadrene then cast a spell that rose a row of the crystal steps up in the path of Muline, but the mighty cat burst through like a cannon ball through glass. Blenadrene could do nothing as Muline was now only a few strides away from him.

"Blenadrene, allow us to help you!" screamed I.

Blenadrene looked towards the young elf bloodied and torn and spoke. "The creator is on our side."

Muline was then there on him, the great Shamual warrior twice the height and many times over the weight of the wizard then palmed Blenadrene by the face and lifted him off of the ground to his eye level and let out a roar that shook the foundation of where they stood. Then he spoke.

"You will now die, wizard, and then I will walk down these steps and kill everyone who has desecrated this holy ground with you!"

The great Shamual warrior who wore a gladiator's armor began to squeeze Blenadrene's head to crush it.

"I will grant you final words, Blenadrene. Speak so that the world will know not to come here."

"You and I will help the world together." said Blenadrene.

Muline looked at Blenadrene very closely. "Wizard, the day of our helping one another will not come for you will not be here to help anyone." Muline began to crush Blenadrene's skull.

Blenadrene began to scream. I then drew his swords and charged Muline. Then there was a loud deep noise that came from the palace that was followed by a purple light that shone from each window and doorway of the palace. Muline dropped Blenadrene and roared to summon all of the Shamual warriors, and they ran up the stairs onto the final steps before the crystal palace at the brief notice, forgetting the battle, and paying no attention to anyone else who was there. They all knelt as the purple light gathered from all the openings and focused through the massive doorway.

I and the others rushed to Blenadrene's body as it lay bleeding and torn.

"Blenadrene, what have you done?" asked I.

"I am paying for my sins, so that Xahmore` might have what it needs to survive the Withering."

"But with your life?" I asked.

"Young one, I have done things in my life that warrant my death, this I do voluntarily because I now know there are more things worth living for than power and orders from a throne. Meeting your mother allowed me to raise a daughter, and seeing you come into the world let me know that there is hope, so as the creator sent us you, I brought you to Ulrant's Palace." Blenadrene said weakly.

"Why?" I asked almost crying.

"Ask him. I am tired now, let me rest." Blenadrene said as he breathed out for the final time.

As Blenadrene closed his eyes, the purple light bent towards his body and a hand lifted his spirit from his body into the air. His spirit stood upon the beam of light illuminated. And a calming voice humbled all who heard it.

"So you returned as I said you would. One of the coldest hearts in all Xahmore` found something he would die for. I thought that you would be willing to die for power until I saw the fear in your eyes before Muline struck you. But now your heart has been warmed and you fight for the love of others and not the conquest of the land. The fear has gone from you, so has the hatred and desire for power. Tell me, Blenadrene, who is it you love so much that you risked putting your puzzle of death back in motion?" asked the voice from the purple light.

Blenadrene pointed to I. "Him, the promise that was made in prophecy." Blenadrene then smiled at I and then looked back to where the light came from. "He and his mother have shown me that the time one puts into others strengthens one's weaknesses, removes sin, and destroys fear."

The light drew back into the palace along with Blenadrene's spirit.

The voice then spoke again. "Muline, my son, bring his body and the black-eyed elf before me."

"Yes, father." Muline answered with no resentment. The massive cat being rose from his knee and walked down the crystal steps toward the three living and one lifeless body.

All the elves in the courtyard and on the bottom of the steps rushed to attack the now morbid Shamual warriors and take the palace. As they reached the middle of the stairs screaming out in barbaric cries for blood, I turned to them and held his hand out.

"Stop!" I said.

The elves all slowed in their charge upon the thirty-second step and gazed upon the blotted black-eyed elf.

"It is him!" said one elf as he dropped his weapon and took a knee with a bowed head.

The rest spoke in amazement and eventually did the same as the first. I then turned to Muline and nodded. Muline then picked up the body of Blenadrene in one hand and draped it over his shoulder.

"Come, elf, that is to save us all, my father wishes to see you." said Muline in a calm and respectful tone.

They walked up the last nineteen of the 360 steps to a flat shimmering surface that stretched a good ways to the massive door of the palace.

"This door looks big enough for the creator to walk through!" I said.

"The creator walking into the side of this mountain is what created this entire palace, young elf." said Muline. "I have not even been permitted to pass this door until now. I have only seen my father once and that was at my creation. Since then I have protected the doorway along with my brothers."

"Why could you not enter the palace?" asked I.

"There was no need apparently, until now. My place is at the door protecting the palace. My duties are my reason for living this life. I was blessed with what I have to protect my father. Not to be under him as a pet is to his master." Muline answered.

"So in essence there is no love only your duty?" I asked.

"I love him dearly, so I repay my debt by performing my duty, and I am willing to give my life to protect his." Muline replied.

"I understand how that feeling ensnares the soul." I said as he thought about his mother. "So has anyone been allowed inside besides us now?"

"Only few, and of those few all but two were dragons." said Muline.

"What did dragons come here for?" the young elf asked.

"To bestow knowledge from all corners of the Xahmore` so that the others would be kept abreast of what was transpiring across the land, thus, enabling them to carry out the creator's wishes, but I have not seen one in almost a thousand years." the Shamual warrior explained.

"So this place where they bestowed knowledge, is it similar to the scribe's den?" I asked.

Muline chuckled slightly, "No young protector it is far greater. Every time one dragon came and bestowed his knowledge, the others became aware. This was made by a power unrivaled by any. It was the creator's way of watching his plan unfold without having to always be involved. But enough talk we are here." Muline said.

As the two reached the door with Blenadrene's body Muline bowed his head and said a brief prayer. I bowed with him.

"Oh great creator, I know your purpose for these events is soon to be revealed to us. We come before you and ask that you would go with us wherever this last step leads us. Thank you." Muline then lifted his head and looked at I with slight tears in his eyes. "Let us go, young elf."

They both took the last step where only the holiest beings had been, and where the most holy had actually walked.

40

BEGIN THE UPRISING

The portal he opened closed then he turned and was back in the darkness. The sound of water dripping through cracks and the agony of moans in the distance filled the pitch black. He breathed heavily, grunting on his exhales because he was tired, angry, and injured.

He walked through the dark and only the noise in front of him signified beings moved from in front of him to let him pass. He walked up five steps, and on the sixth, he reached the plateau of a huge hexagon with steps on each side.

His eyes began to glow red, he walked to the center of the hexagon and raised his right hand and the room illuminated in the purple hue around the partially clothed blotted elf he had in his raised hand.

Yorenzana had returned to show the prize the demons had so long waited for. The illumination filled the room and pushed the darkness back to reveal an army of demons dressed and armed for war.

"Behold the carrier of the shard!" Yorenzana yelled out in victory.

The cavern full of demons all yelled in delight knowing that the day had come that they would free their master from bondage and rule over Xahmore`. They were in such euphoria over the death and destruction to come, they began to slaughter the smaller demons.

"Yes, my brothers, the time of The Withering is upon us and we can not be stopped!" Yorenzana yelled insanely.

The cavern once again roared in delight.

"My wounds will heal in a few days time and then we will walk upon the surface to free our master and burn Xahmore`, and those responsible for his imprisonment will die!" he yelled.

Yorenzana then released the female blotted elf, and she floated to the ceiling and was pent there, arms stretched out and legs together as a cross.

A huge, red four-horned demon who could almost see eye to eye with Yorenzana then walked up to address the demon wizard.

"Brother, when will we begin our march to the gate of the dragons?" asked the demon.

"Begin your march at dawn, Kremlin, I will meet you there in three days with the elfin girl. Kill anything that stands in your way." Yorenzana ordered.

"Consider it done." The demon said as he walked away dragging a huge, bloody spiked club into the darkness.

41

Knowledge of Dawn

The inside of the palace was an awesome sight. The crystal walls were smooth and clear. They entered a vast room that took up almost the entire inside of the palace. There were no flags, no court of nobles, no statues, nor trophies or monuments; there was only a purple hue coming from the far side of the room that filled the crystal walls.

Muline and I walked forth with Blenadrene's body.

I, who was taken by the beautiful purple illumination, stopped just short of where Muline walked to and watched.

"Father, we have come at your request." said Muline as he took one knee and bowed his head. "What would you have us do?"

"Watch and listen." said a calming voice. "Young protector, please step forward so that you may see these visions clearly."

I did as Ulrant said and stepped forward. Both of their eyes started to glow the purple hue as if no eyes where present within their skulls. Their minds rose to the place where Ulrant sat and they did not move.

Ulrant began to speak to both of their minds and showed them things as he spoke.

"Since the dawn of life on this world, there has been a battle that has been waged behind the reality that everyone has seen.

"The beast, as it is known to most, lived among the creator for eons before he created anything else. It journeyed with the creator as the heavens where created. It watched as stars, comets, suns, and space was formed.

"This planet was molded by the creator, and he created to dwell in it what are now called dragons. The creator taught the dragons everything they should know in order to maintain this planet and watch over all he would create. Then he created me in order to keep and link the knowledge of the dragons and all they did and observed. But we, like the comet and the stars, were bound by a code of order that made us act upon duty and order. As the sun rose to light the world, we performed our duties without question.

"Then the creator in his greatness made life that had a choice to do what it felt on impulse and passion. He created the elfin race and they like us were immortal, but they lived a life that was not connected to duty alone. They danced, they fellowshipped, they loved, they felt emotions, they reproduced, they created art, they created music, and continued to create things to better their lives. The creator spoke with them daily and was pleased with the world he had created.

"The beast thought that this was unfair to all things created before the elves and that this freedom to think freely along with immortality made them as the creator was. In an attempt to show the creator that this creation was an abomination and would do wrong with the gift given it, the beast left the heavens and dwelled amongst the elves, showing them magic and telling them of the heavens. It showed them what beauty was and began to separate them with insecurity and envy. It showed some of them how to gain the advantage over others and created wars among them, and in turn there was the first living thing to be killed.

"This made the creator sad with the elfin race and angry with the beast. They both were punished. The elves were forced to share a world created for them with races that would not be immortal but be bigger, stronger, and more barbaric than the elves and have just as much freedom as they. This made the world dangerous and full of turmoil. Since these beings would not be able to live forever, they would do whatever was necessary to live life as lavish as they could before their time ended. This world was so much more beautiful before that time came.

"The beast was banished from the heavens for meddling in the creator's work. It was placed under the same restrictions that all created life on this planet was. It had great power and limited space in which to possess it in. The beast became miserable and began to hate the creator for locking him inside such a small space. Tens of thousands of years living in its anger and frustration, it began to destroy the world. Entire races were wiped from the world. Wars were started which destroyed entire civilizations. Knowledge was distorted and the world became blind.

"Then the beast guided them to its ways of judgment, jealousy, greed, and envy. In turn its teachings lead to stealing, killing, and false power. This pleased the beast.

"The creator did not leave the races he created in all peril. He gave those who had good hearts help and sent the dragons upon the beast to seal him into an even smaller place that would cause him more misery and frustration. Most of the dragons died in the battle to trap it but the last seven succeeded. The beast though had followers and they searched for the way to free it from the prison made by the dragons, and one by one suffered the same fate.

"The world continued on this path of evil and has lead back to the beast returning to freedom upon the face of Xahmore`. It wants revenge, and once free, it will release its power and minions to slay the world. The Withering will happen but some of the lives spared will be the ones to finally destroy the beast."

Ulrant then released the hold he had on the minds of the two in front of him.

"With this, you must save who you can and end the Withering. Go. The demon army is already marching towards Emolia." said Ulrant.

I and Muline left the presence of Ulrant with purpose.

"Now…" spoke Ulrant to the spirit of Blenadrene, "let me tell you secrets of the new and old."

42

Eyes of Oolantoo

"There was one who saw the most horrific disfiguring of Xahmore` take place and lived to tell of it, his name was Oolantoo. This portion of my story was passed down through the generations of his tribe the Kwilamy. I was lucky enough to hear it told by one of them."

"Wise elder, I thought the Kwilamy all died in the war of souls?" asked Lorimeck.

"Almost all of them did, but a few migrated away from their homeland before that war. One of them told me this story."

"Is it going to be scary?" asked Feloshia.

"It may be a little gruesome, little one" I said with a light smile.

"Great!!" she replied.

"Tell us of what Oolantoo saw, wise elder." pleaded Lorimeck.

"As you wish."

In the great forest of Goondrach, the wildlife was busy following nature's course. The trees stood majestic, looking as if they reached for the heavens. The ground displayed some of the most brilliantly colored shrubbery and flowers. The soil here was the greatest for any life to thrive. There were four lakes that provided water for the thousands of species that called the great wood home. And this was just the portion known to us.

Oolantoo was a human spirit-talker who found the great forest and frequented it for herbs and shrub for potions. These woods represented the beauty and vast life of Xahmore˚ untouched by the races' buildings and war. I guess that is why they chose that place to preface the Withering of Xahmore˚.

The day it all happened started as the most beautiful of days. The warmth of the sun caressed the wood. The smell in the air was of fresh bloomed ganelia flowers. The song of the narisha birds seemed to serenade the world.

Slowly the song began to dwindle away, and a horrible stench captivated the air, overtaking the freshness of the wood and it became extremely cold. Every bird lifted from the trees and flew away. All manner of animal, small and quick to large and cumbersome, seemed to all at once begin to head west. Oolantoo shifted into a spirit form knowing that danger must be approaching. What happened next was described by him as death by the hand of hell.

He watched a single leaf fall from a tree, and as it reached eye level with him, it stopped its descent. It then froze. Oolantoo backed away. The leaf looked as if it had been in the snowy mountains of Lomdell. The ice from the leaf then began to spread into the air, appearing to freeze everything behind it. Oolantoo said that it looked as if the ice spread and became a great window that divided the forest in half. It stretched to the top of the enormous trees and dug deep into the ground.

Then there was a huge thud as if something gigantic was stomping the land. Oolantoo said it made the ground shake beneath him. Then there was another that shook the smaller trees to the ground. The third thud cracked the ice, and Oolantoo moved from it and took a space behind a huge rock a few hundred feet from the wall of ice. The next thud sent a chunk of ice flying through the forest, smashing onto the ground showing that it was something behind the ice hitting it.

Oolantoo became afraid and moved back further and off to the right from where the crack in the ice was. He had never seen something so awesome. His fear warranted him to leave, but such a sight intrigued him to stay. There was a muffled roar from behind the ice that was followed by a muffled response of what sounded like thousands roaring in reply. Then the most horrific site that Oolantoo had seen engulfed his eyes.

The final thud revealed a huge spiked club and the wall off ice came down smashing upon the land. Fire and blood rushed through the forest as thousands of demons raced from behind the ice where they had already slain one half of the forest and left its animals and vegetation dead and burning.

Oolantoo watched as they moved swiftly and began to destroy everything they could see. Trees were bashed, animals were eaten live, and all was set on fire. The sky began to become black with soot. The screams of the animals were horrid, the bigger ones stopped running and tried to fight back but were overtaken and slaughtered.

The scene was so dreadful, Oolantoo was paralyzed with fear. The demons moved around him like locusts in a windstorm. They all were oblivious to him watching, or so it seemed.

"Human." said Kremlin.

Oolantoo turned to see the huge red demon standing directly behind him.

"K-K-K-Kremlin." stuttered Oolantoo.

"You know of me. Good. That means you know why I am here." the red demon said.

All of the demons began to gather in battalion formations behind Kremlin.

"You will carry this orb toward the Emolian Empire and will not stop until you are inside the throne room of Telaris Emolian." Kremlin commanded.

Oolantoo turned back into his human form entranced, and his eyes began to glow red. Another demon stepped forth and handed him an orb the size of a small pumpkin that had what appeared to be at least a hundred eyes in it.

"I will do as you have commanded." he replied to Kremlin.

"Good, now go!" Kremlin instructed the human.

Oolantoo then turned east and walked holding the orb of eyes out in front of him.

Kremlin then snarled and turned to a lesser demon.

"Velono, you and a battalion of carnivores stay here and burn what we have not. While you wait for them, kill who you can."

"Yes, Kremlin!" he answered.

The demon who appeared as a humanoid being of molten rock turned to a group of sleek, dark, smooth-skinned demons that were shaking and drooling disgusting amounts of saliva from large sharp teeth and spoke harshly.

"Fan out and destroy anything you can find until I call for you."

The five hundred or so demons moved quickly through the burning forest bouncing from tree to tree laughing as hyenas do.

"Let us march to Emolia!" bellowed Kremlin.

The demon army roared. Kremlin then mounted a death lizard and motioned his arm that held the spiked club forward. The demon army began its march.

43

ARMY OF LIGHT

All eyes remained fixed on the great doorway that I and Muline walked into. There were mixed emotions among the Shamual and the warriors of the Emolian Empire. The blotted elf had finally shown himself as prophecy said he would. The summoning of him and Muline into the palace of Ulrant were but signs of a troubling time they would have to deal with. Not aware that the battle ready armies already stood there on the steps awaiting the call for war—the war.

"What do you think is happening in there?" asked Mlar.

"I am not sure but I hope it is beneficial to us all." answered Rimleon. "Yorenzana will not wait to long to free the beast, so this time should not be wasted."

Just as the legendary general finished his statement, a voice from the elves on the steps below yelled out.

"Look, they have returned!!"

I and Muline walked to the edge of the top step. Muline then spoke to his people.

"My brothers, we have defended this palace for tens of thousands of years. It is now time to defend it along with the rest of Xahmore`. The very thing that we have been created to fight against will tear the world apart soon, and we must do our best to save who we can so that in the days ahead of this, we all can rise and strike down this evil. Let us not tarry, let us not fear, and let us not be concerned with anything but the purging of this evil from our existence once and for all. Are you with me?" Muline said as he raised his right paw into the air, calling his people to arms.

A furious roar came from the Shamual, as all equally raised their right paw in agreement of their brother's speech.

I then walked down to the elves below.

"Sons of Emolia, you have been misled since time became a factor in life. The emperor you serve has been under the spell of a demon named Yorenzana for his entire term. All the missions you have been sent on, all the land you have claimed, all that you have slaughtered, and all of your fallen comrades have been in the name of evil. The mission you were sent here for was to seek out Ulrant to gain knowledge on how to free Yorenzana's master, the beast." The blotted black-eyed elf said.

Most of the army looked towards each other in disbelief. Some screamed out and began to cry. Others kept their eyes on the blotted elf.

"You mean to tell us our lives have been lies all these years? Why should we believe you?" shouted one soldier.

"Search your heart warrior. Does it not feel somewhat empty? Did it not all make sense as to why you felt that way when I told you the truth?" replied I.

The warrior hung his head in shame.

"What are we to do? We only know what we have been! How can we make up for the tyranny and murder we have committed in the name of the beast?" yelled another warrior.

"You are the army of Blenadrene, the Lord of War, you are among the best warriors in the history of Xahmore`, and destiny has spared you to now redeem yourselves by helping to right the greatest wrong of all. You can wallow in self-pity but it will do you no good. You can relieve your mind from your sins by falling on your sword, or relish in the truth I have given you and wield your sword to now help save instead of destroy. Which will it be?" asked the young elf.

The elves looked around to one another for a few moments. Then one of the most decorated elves, Evangel, raised his broad sword. They all then raised their weapons to the sky and said nothing. I stood and looked out upon the massive army of thousands and then looked back to his friends.

"This means that they will fight until the last one of them has no voice to cry out war. This means they will die for the cause laid out before them." said Rimleon as he raised his right gauntlet and conjured a soul spear.

Mlar then raised his lance. I turned to the army and removed one of his swords and raised it to the sky. The army then began to shout and sing praises to the creator.

Then the palace glowed, and Ulrant spoke so that they all could hear him.

"I pronounce you the Army of Light. You are the ones who will stand in this dark time to protect Xahmore`. Some of you will give your very lives and some of you will live forever in legend. Some of you will even be there the day the beast is struck to the depths. Now, I return to you your general. May the creator help us."

Then all of the purple hue channeled into the great doorway and a tall dark slim figure walked through, donning a robe that was purple and trimmed in gold. Blenadrene walked on to the first step and looked over the army of Shamual and Elf at his command. A gust of wind moved over the army. Blenadrene placed his hands together as if to pray and bowed his head.

"Thank you." whispered Blenadrene softly.

As the wind dissipated, he raised his hands and spoke.

"Army of Light," he bellowed with an undeniable confidence, "let us prepare for war!!

The army answered back with the loudest of cries.

44

LORD OF WAR

The Army of Light had been broken into five battalions of seven hundred. Each battalion was three-parts elf and one-part Shamual except two. They all were lined in ten by ten formations in the large fields high above Xahmore outside of the crystal city. They stood as disciplined as statues while a light breeze caressed the brown grass that surrounded them. Some of the faces showed to be uneasy about fate, others eager for redemption.

All eyes were forward upon the front of the field where I stood with Rimleon, Mlar, and Muline. There were five large portals opening in front of Blenadrene who turned to the army and spoke.

"The time has come for us to embrace our destinies. Some of us will die this day, some of us the next, but let your last breath not be in vain. Let the spirit leave your body knowing you opposed the greatest of evils. Worry not of death because it is written that we will win in the days ahead. Our mission now is to save as many lives as we can, so that the stand can be made in the future to destroy the beast. I have been told that there are powerful beings that must live through the Withering and some of you will be responsible for them for they will in some way shape our future. These portals will take you to your assigned posts for this horrid time. May the creator watch over you."

Blenadrene then walked to each respective battalion and gave instruction and blessing to each commander. All battalions except the two with one-part elf and three-part Shamual walked into the portals.

"What are we to do, Blenadrene?" asked I.

"Look at the horizon to the south. Do you see the smoke, young elf?"

"Yes, faintly. Right on the horizon I see the smoke." I said.

"That is the trail you and Muline will follow. Mlar and Rimleon will accompany you along with the remaining battalions."

"Where does it lead, Blenadrene?"

"To the one you love the most, I."

"What about you?" asked Rimleon.

"There is an old friend that I must go see. He has needed my help for a while. I will wait here until it is time for me to visit him. Do not worry, I will see you in a few days." Blenadrene assured.

"Let us go, I, we must not waste any more time." said Muline.

Blenadrene then extended his hands and opened another portal that smelled with death and burning wood, and the 1404 walked into it and it sealed.

He then sat cross-legged in the air and began to meditate.

45

SMOKE

They walked into a smoke as thick as fog on the sea. Flames could still be heard crackling away at wood and flapping in the wind. It was hard to breath. They began to cough frantically. There was a wizard or two in their midst who cleared the air where they stood so that they could breathe amongst the inferno-ridden land.

They all cleared their lungs of the inhaled burnings and looked out and saw the destruction that surrounded them.

"By the creator's breath, what did this?" asked Rimleon as he approached the smoke.

"This was done by the army led by Kremlin, the beast's general of war." said an old elf wizard who stood next to the smoke.

"How do you know this, old one?"

"I have read the scrolls of the recorders. The prophecy said that upon the beast's return the untouched beauty will be desecrated by the warlord of the beast. This must have been the most beautiful place in all Xahmore`." the old wizard said.

"Shhh." said I, "Did you hear that?"

"What?" answered Rimleon.

"Sounds like laughter of some sort." I said.

The faint sound began to get closer to their position. The Shamual started to growl softly.

"Muline, what is it?" asked I.

"I do not know. The smoke clouds my sense of smell, but it sounds as if we are not alone in the least bit." he growled.

"Prepare yourselves!" yelled Rimleon.

The laughter was right beyond the smoke. The old wizard walked to the edge of the smoke and waved his hand in order to clear it. The smoke lightened to a mist, and he saw a face that smiled at him with huge razor-like teeth with saliva dripping from them. He screamed out and was snatched into the smoke.

"Demons!" yelled Muline.

The warriors all turned to the smoke that surrounded them and drew their weapons and readied spells.

The laughter began to surround them.

Every few seconds someone would get snatched into the smoke and cry out in pain.

"Enough of this, prepare to kill or be killed!" yelled Rimleon as he smashed his gauntlets together causing the smoke to be blown back and the hundreds of sleek, dark carnivore demons to jump in on the army of elves and Shamual.

The demons took many lives due to the initial quick attack, but once the element of surprise was gone, they never stood a chance.

The warriors, who had battled the fiercest forces and conquered the most rugged lands combined, with the Shamual, who had protected Ulrant for lifetimes against the most powerful of beings, obliterated most of the mindless killers within minutes. The rest ran away but did not make it far before they were run down and killed.

The army let out a roar of victory!

"Let's move," commanded Rimleon, "There are probably more of them out there or worse out among common folk."

"It is not the common folk you should be concerned with, elf," said a voice from within the further reaches of the smoke.

The warriors looked to where the voice echoed from and saw a figure that began to glow a bright red.

"I." Muline called for his comrade but got no answer, nor did he see the blotted black-eyed elf in the ranks.

The glow from the figure in the smoke became brighter and brighter by the moment accompanied by a loud hum. The figure laughed as fire started to radiate from within his body out towards the army of light. The smoke then began to swirl as if the wind was blowing. The heat from the growing fire began to reach the warriors. They tried long range attacks but all where caught up in the flame and burned, weapon and spell alike.

"Are you all ready to die?" asked the glowing figure as he concentrated and became bright as the sun itself and the flame raised towards the army.

There was a gust of wind and the smoke then seemed to split down the middle, clearing a path towards the glowing figure. Then as the smoke reached the flame, the fire all flowed to the front of the clearing in the smoke and as the path cut through the smoke reached the glowing figure there was a bright flash. All warriors covered their eyes. The brightness began to dim.

"What happened?" asked Muline.

"Look into the path cleared in the smoke and see." said Rimleon.

There at the end of the path, was I crouching on the other side of a demon body that laid in three pieces? He held his swords out to his sides with the flame of the demon still on them. He rose from his crouch and lifted the swords to his face and spoke to the flame harshly.

"Take me to Kremlin!"

He then crossed the swords in an x and raked them across each other viciously, and the flame that spewed out as a dragon's head moved all around in front of the elf until it slowed then moved hurriedly toward the south. I looked back at the army, pulled his hood over his dreadlocks, and darted off behind the flame.

"To destiny!" yelled Muline as he took on all fours and ran off behind I with the entire army yelling and running behind him with the path cleared by the one sent to protect them all.

46

BETWEEN FRIENDS

Blenadrene after a day of meditation stepped down to the ground. He looked out to the horizon and saw that the smoke had cleared. *Good job, my boy.* He thought. He then opened a portal small in size that he had to duck to walk into. After he stepped through, he heard the soft music of a harp, the sweet melody of a chime, and the gentle song of a beautiful voice. He walked to that side of the room.

"You all have been playing this tune for a long while have you not?" Blenadrene said with smile. "How about playing something else?"

There was no response.

"Which one of you is it?" he asked nicely.

There was no response, just the soft music. He looked at them all closely to see the harp was part of the player's shoulder, as well as the chime was part of the players hand. He also noticed that the songstress's feet where infused to the floor.

"I see. It must be all three of you. I am sorry." Blenadrene apologized.

They did not respond but looked to him with tears in their eyes which spilled over onto their faces.

"I cannot undo this spell without destroying you, but you will be free from this prison. Do you understand me?" he asked.

They began to play and sing with the grandest of emotion and passion.

"Good. May the creator guide your souls." he responded to them.

Blenadrene then spoke a few words that turned them all to statues. He then clinched his fist and the statues crumbled to dust. He spoke a few more words and the dust dissolved into the floor. The spell was undone.

"Blenadrene, my old friend, is that really you?" a voice bellowed out in glee.

"Yes, Telaris, it is." Blenadrene smiled and walked towards his friend.

"I have been waiting a long time for you to return, but for some reason I cannot remember why." Telaris said with a confused look on his face.

"How old are you?" asked Blenadrene.

"1500 years. Why do you ask such a childish question?" Telaris asked.

"You are almost twice that age sire. Things have transpired that have had you in a delusional state for a while, and I need to inform you as best I can. The days ahead are filled with death and destruction, and we were used to bring it to this point." The wizard said with heavy emotion.

Blenadrene told Telaris of all the things that transpired while he had been under the spell of the music. Telaris cried great tears of great pain and sorrow.

"What have we done?" he asked Blenadrene.

"What we have done is nothing, but what has been our destiny, you had no control. I believed that I was honoring you until the truth was brought to me by Ulrant." He answered.

"Now what do we do?" Telaris asked.

Blenadrene placed his arm around his friend and walked him to the window that looked out on the vast land.

"This will be destroyed. Hopefully, we will survive." Blenadrene said.

"Why are they coming here first?" asked Telaris.

"They will come to open that?" Blenadrene pointed to the floor that had a huge emblem of numerous dragons flying around on it. "When this palace was built, it was built around this huge doorway that the dragons made to seal the beast behind. Yorenzana has the power he needs to open it now, and it will happen within the next day."

"What will we do, Blenadrene?"

Blenadrene looked out the window to the west.

"I don't know, but we will need to evacuate as many as we can, rally the army, and fight until help arrives." said the Lord of War.

"Help? What manner of being can help us against the beast and his horde?" Telaris asked, doubtful that there was such a being.

"There is one thing I didn't tell you, old friend. Fate allowed me to cross paths with the blotted elf that has the black eyes. I raised him as my own grandson. He is now behind the demon army that approaches Emolia and will be here ready to slay each and every demon he must to reach this room." Blenadrene said with a slight smile.

"What makes you so sure he will fight with such intent?" asked the emperor.

"The key to this door that the demon wizard has," Blenadrene turned to Telaris," is within his mother!"

47

CHASING DEATH

The dark night was lit by a ball of fire that was shaped like a dragon's head. It followed a path marred by destruction and death. Burned villages, destroyed woods, raped bodies, obliterated crops—all a sign of things to come. I followed the speeding dragons head from one village to the next. All things that the demon army passed, they destroyed. I thought of his mother as he ran, knowing she is in the midst of this evil.

He stepped in puddles of blood leaped through walls of fire, and hurdled piles of the dead. He thought nothing of it, just of his mother.

Demons where left in his path to try and stop his progress. Some powerful, some in packs, but he killed them all with ease. The focus on saving his mother had enhanced his power, and he used every bit of it as he slew every demon left in his way.

There was but one demon that even slowed I down.

I came to a town known as Delhora. A slender demon with a staff stood in the middle of the burning town. I reached where the demon stood and halted his run with his hooded frame inches away from the demon.

Dust, soot, and flames fanned around as I stopped.

"Hello, elf, I am Blad." said the demon.

"Do you wish to perish as your brothers have, Blad?"

"No, I just wish to test your skill and mine as well. I have no desire to be killed. I am not as foolish as my brothers. I know the time comes for us to rule Xahmore`, why miss out? I just simply want to…spar."

"I have not the time for this, demon!"

"Surely you could find time for a quick match." Said Blad as the flame I followed was halted and then duplicated by Blad. "Besides, you don't know your way from here."

"And if I do not spar, demon?"

"Then let's just say by the time you find out which flame is the right one, your beautiful mother would be in a bit of a bind." the demon smiled.

I removed his hood and the cloak vanished to reveal a hardened look on his youthful face. His brow sweaty from the intense running and a few of his dreads hung in front of his face. He was holding the staff that the blind Orc had given him.

"You are but a child." Blad said in a surprised tone.

"I have wasted enough time with you, demon!" I said in an angered voice as he attacked Blad.

He attacked in arrays of ways and Blad blocked every strike. I was enraged and fought harder. Blad still blocked the staff and maintained poise. Then I stepped back and charged and attacked at such a speed, there appeared to be two of him. Blad could not block all the blows. He was struck several times and the last swing of I's staff knocked Blad from his feet onto his backside.

The demon stood with a smile and directed to I the correct flame to follow and motioned his hand forward and the flame raced yet again.

"If this flame does not take me to Kremlin, I will be back to kill you." said I with conviction.

"Do not fret, young elf, I send you on the right path, besides you will do me a favor when you get there." the demon said.

I then sprinted off behind the flame now headed east.

Then there was a voice in the air who spoke to Blad.

"The elf has passed you and you live, why is this so?"

"I have my reasons, Kremlin."

"I will deal with you and your games later!" Kremlin threatened.

"Well, my brother, I don't think I am who you should be worried about." Blad began to snicker.

There was a long deep grunt.

"Good-bye, Kremlin." Blad said as he began to laugh uncontrollably.

48

WHO WILL STAND

After Blenadrene had enlightened Telaris, the emperor of the elves sent word for all warriors to come to the palace and for all others to evacuate the city to the north and south portions of the kingdom.

Once the orders had been carried out, an army formed and all others began to leave. On the great plains that lay to the east wall of the castle stood an army of elves that numbered at least twenty thousand. They stood together, mercenary and knight, common magician and the most decorated wizard, barbarian and elite guard.

To the north and south gates of the city saw hundreds of thousands of elves leaving the city: the elderly, the young, woman, and men who had no special ability and those who would preserve the history of what was before and then.

"My kingdom walks unto its death," said Telaris.

"No, your kingdom leaves from death, so that it may return one day," said Blenadrene. "They stand a better chance against all of Xahmore' than they do here when the sun rises on the morrow. The kingdom is more than the people, buildings, and artifacts. The kingdom is all those things and more combined."

"The inhabitants of the walls are like the blood of the body, and the blood now exits from the wound made by our mistakes." Telaris said as a failure.

"Yes, this is true, but this is destiny's own design. We are just the players on a larger stage and our parts were written to be as they are. Now we have the chance to better our portion of the story. The blood will return to the body, but only after the disease has been cut out." Blenadrene said to his friend.

"Well, the poison of the serpent has infected the body and we were the fangs? So it is only right that when the venom comes to claim life, we are here to stop it from doing so." Telaris said as he approached the terrace to address his warriors.

"More life will be claimed than should be, old friend, but not in its entirety." Blenadrene said after Telaris left the chamber.

He took a deep breath and followed the emperor to stand at his side as he addressed the army.

"Elves," Telaris bellowed to the thousands below, "We are in a low point in our history. The time of the Withering is upon us."

The crowd began to talk amongst themselves some. Telaris then quieted them and spoke again.

"As the first race, we are to blame and it is time for us to take up for what was given to us, and if is seen fit...to pay for our sins. There are approaching dangers that will come from all sides once the sun rises again. Already the air fills with the scent of burning flesh. You will have the beast's great army at your front, and the beast itself at your back. But we will have the Creator's promise of victory on our sides. Just as we have conquered lands and destroyed the fiercest armies, we will defeat this evil and look down on its carcass as it burns! We fight this fight for survival of our families, for our kind, for Emolia, for all Xahmore!"

The gathered yelled out a battle cry that could be heard by the first elves who exited the city long ago. But this cry did not only fall on elfin ears.

The sun set to the west and the warriors set camp on the north plain of the palace. When the sun had completely submerged behind the far off hills of Bluelynd, there was an eerie glow to the hills of the west as if the sun had caught the other side of the world on fire.

"They are near." said Blenadrene to Telaris.

"Yes, and in great number." Telaris motioned to one of the guards inside the throne room. "Go amongst the gathered and seek out Dark Soul and have him come and bring his guild. We will need swift swords and mighty magic inside this room on the morrow."

The guard left the room in search of the elf.

"Dark Soul, my lord?" inquired Blenadrene. "The elite guard turned mercenary?"

"He and his guild were not mercenaries by chance. I order them to be so that I would know most of the plotting in Xahmore`, for who would be hired but the best. They never were stripped of their armor as the story goes."

"You are wise, old friend. Let's hope he is there."

"Oh he is Blenadrene. Emolia is his mother. He beckons to her call like a sailor to a siren. There will be a great battle this sunrise. One that will be told of until the end, and then told of when the Creator starts it all again. Let us prepare ourselves."

The guard reached the camp outside the palace in search of the legendary elf and his guild. Through many tent-like structures and mini campsites he searched. He came across many powerful elves but none was the one he was sent for. Then a beautiful female elf came to him.

"Hello." she said with a smile. "Are you looking for someone?"

"Yes, I am searching for Dark soul, do you know of him?" he asked.

Her smile went away. She looked over her left shoulder. The guard took his eye off her and looked over her shoulder, and she was under his neck quickly with a small blade.

"Why do you search for him?" she asked ruthlessly.

"Telaris sent me to find him. He requests his presence in the throne room." The guard said quickly.

"I don't know if I believe you. You could be someone who wants to use this opportunity to assassinate him." the female elf said.

"Enough!" a voice spoke loudly corralling all eyes and ears in the area. "Guard, how do you know Dark Soul is here among us?"

"I don't. Telaris said that he would be because Emolia is his mother and he beckons to her call." said the guard.

"Release him Mahalia. Tell Telaris that Dark Soul has heard his mother and will be there before the sun rises." said the stranger.

49

THE DAWN

The dark was quiet. Silent to the point that existence itself seemed unreal. There was no wind, no wild noise, not even the sound of anyone breathing broke the silence. It was as if the world was bracing itself for what would become it.

"Where is he?" asked a deep voice.

"He is a thousand paces away from their front lines, brother." An answer came from a voice just as dark.

"Gooooood. I will meet you in the throne room to release our master. Don't tarry, it could be costly." The deep voice said again.

"I will be there, Yorenzana. The elves will not hold us back." Kremlin answered.

"Tell me, brother, did any of the ones you left behind to confront him ever make it back to their ranks?" the demon wizard asked of his brother.

"I would have been disappointed if they had." Kremlin said in a slightly worried tone.

"Surely you would have." Yorenzana said slyly.

"The sun rises. It is time." alerted Kremlin.

The sun began to rise in the east and the elfin army stood ready for battle. As the sunlight made its way over the eastern plain of the palace and the darkness crept back towards the hill. There was no demon army, only a human walking towards the elves with something in his outstretched hands.

"Stranger approaches!" yelled the lookout atop the palace.

A lieutenant looked through his telescope at the stranger to see he was human and possessed. He passed the telescope to his commander so that he may see.

"It is time," the general said as he took the scope from his eye. "Stop and identify yourself!" screamed the general of the elite guard.

Oolantoo could do neither.

"Archers!" screamed the general, "Ready your arrows!"

"No, no, no, no, no." said a tired bloodied Oolantoo as he got closer to the army.

"Aim!" the general ordered.

"Please, no." Oolantoo said as loud as his weakened body would allow.

"Fire!" the general commanded.

"Creator, help us." Oolantoo said as he watched the arrows blanket the sky towards him.

The orb of eyes he held began to glow blue. As the first arrow reached him, it was deflected back into the sky by the glow and was now itself blue. Every arrow that had been fired followed suit. The sky was now full of the enchanted arrows that flew back and struck each archer dead.

"First line, take him down!" yelled the general fiercely.

The fist line of infantry moved in to intercept the human. He tried to warn them but they paid no mind as they closed in on him. The first warrior to reach him raised his sword above his head to strike down and one eye from the orb released the huge death lizard that bit the elfin warrior in two and began to eat him. On the lizard's back was the beast's warlord, Kremlin. The orb of eyes then glowed red and just behind him suddenly was the army of demons killing and devouring the first wave of elves sent to destroy Oolantoo.

"Die!" Kremlin said to the army of elves as he motioned Oolantoo forward and then signaled for the demon army to attack.

"For Xahmore`!" yelled the general as he flipped down the faceplate on his helmet and charged the demons with the 20,000 elves right behind him.

From the balcony Blenadrene and Telaris watched.

"The end of the world as we know it has come, my friend." said Telaris as he looked out at the massive demon army that seemed to cover the horizon.

"Yes, it has, but the world is not the number of living but how they survive." Blenadrene said.

They both turned and walked into the throne room. There stood five elves dressed in brown leather and adorned with the rarest of weapons.

"Mahalia, make sure nothing comes through that balcony door." ordered Telaris. "Goreem, Soleah, and Laulare support the guard at the main entrance to this chamber." They all answered, "Yes, sire," as they manned their designated post.

"What about me, my lord, how may I serve Emolia, possibly for my last time?" said a tall, brown elf with brown eyes and long dreads that hung to his chest.

"Dark Soul you will stand in front of the Dragon's door with Blenadrene and myself. Yorenzana will have to fight this day to release the beast back upon the land."

"Yes, my lord." Dark Soul said as he bowed his head to Telaris.

I

The first set of swords then touched and could be heard amongst the hooves pounding and the battle cries. Then the next set, then two more, then five, then the clashes began to sound as metal rain on stone streets.

It was not long after the first scream of life leaving a body was heard. The scream was the most horrid any within an ear shot had heard. Demons and elf alike began to fall and bleed upon the western plain of the palace. The canvas for the death of the world was being primed.

50

WEARY STEPS

Spears flew past his head. His clothes were partially torn and slightly burned. Dirt had collected on the majority of his skin. His eyes were bloodshot and full of tears. He was weak. He was hungry. He was on the verge of death. He could not stop walking.

He stepped over an elfin boy that could not have been anymore that fifty years old and now laid there shaking with his face split open on the right side. He wanted to stop and help the boy, but he kept walking.

He took a few more steps and to his right there was a female warrior who stood over her wounded lover as they were surrounded by demons. She screamed out as to invite the demons to death. He wanted to help her fight them off, but he kept walking.

He stepped in a pool of blood that ran from demons that were being slaughtered by an elf who held two thin swords and moved as swift as humming bird. The blood was hot and burned his feet and lower legs, but the pain did not overtake the joy he had from seeing the demons fall. He wanted to cheer the swordsman on, but he kept walking.

Swords clanged together less that inches from his face, body parts landed next to him, blood splattered on him countless times adding to the filth that was already upon him. He then reached the middle of the elfin formation.

"Stop or I will be forced to kill you, human." said an unusually large elf.

"I cannot," Oolantoo weakly responded, "please kill me."

He kept walking.

The huge elf charged the human with a double-edged axe. Oolantoo smiled as if he knew his suffering was about to end. And as the elf reached him the orb turned blue and sent out a wave of energy that blew every elf and demon down within 100 feet of him. A tear fell from his eye and he kept walking.

As he got closer to the palace, he noticed an elfin female protecting the terrace. She was beautiful and by the way she thwarted demons from the door, she was equally as dangerous. She fought with a short slim blade and if she became overwhelmed with attackers she would sing a high note and they would be knocked from the balcony. He kept walking.

The steps Oolantoo took had now cleared a path that the demon warlord and his lackeys had now begun to march into. Oolantoo knew they were behind him but there was nothing he could do but keep walking.

He reached the wall. He thought surely this would halt his progress. Then without missing a beat he stepped up on the side of the palace and walked as if he were standing on the ground itself. He cried and the tears ran into his ears. He reached the bottom of the balcony and stepped onto it, and he was looking to where he had come from. He could see the entire battle taking place. He saw the warlord of the demons riding his lizard through the path he had cleared and right before he reached the edge and turned parallel to the ground, he looked out and saw the horizon and where the last bit of darkness almost faded away. It looked as if the shadows cried a lone tear that rolled down a hill in the distance. He kept walking.

His tears turned red and burned his eardrums so that he went deaf. This hurt him so bad that as weak as he was, he screamed in pain but could not hear himself. He stepped up on to the banister and on to the balcony.

The female elf looked at the human then the orb he carried.

"I know that orb, human. It is the orb of eyes, whose eyes are those in it?" Mahalia asked.

He said nothing. He kept walking.

She attacked but could not break the barrier the orb of eyes had around Oolantoo. She sang loudly but the hot tears had taken the human's hearing away and he was not captivated nor affected by her song. He kept walking.

She tried one last time to attack and the orb illuminated red. She was levitated and hurled into the throne room where she landed at the feet of Dark Soul.

"Are you okay, Mahalia?" he asked.

She nodded.

Oolantoo continued his walk until he was just beyond the balcony entrance. He stopped.

"No." he said as he fell to the floor in exhaustion and released the orb.

The orb fell to the ground and rolled to the edge of the Dragon's door a few paces from Blenadrene. Dark Soul walked over with his weapon drawn to try and destroy it.

"No! Don't touch it. If you are not more powerful than the last being to touch it, they will be able to control you. Those eyes are not his." screamed Mahalia.

Blenadrene then looked at the orb closely.

"I know those eyes." said Blenadrene.

"Yes, you know them well, my loyal servant." said a deep booming voice.

"Yorenzana," Blenadrene said with a killer's stare, "the beast's lord of magic is here."

He took a stance for battle. The rest of the elves all followed suit and prepared.

Oolantoo passed out, uncertain if he would open his eyes again. His exhausted body could stay conscious no longer, his walk had finally ended.

51

THE SHADOW'S TEAR

Darkness, is it void? Is it absence of light? Is it what covers what we fear or is it the shadow of what waits to consume us? Darkness is always driven away by the light, or is it darkness that eases away so that its younger brother can see what he already knows and will know again? Darkness is always present even when light is prevalent. Darkness needs no surface to reflect it, it just is. Darkness surrounds light. It holds it. It funnels it. It channels it, and it focuses light so that light may have an effect. Darkness does not belong to evil. Evil is trapped by the darkness, so that light may prevail. Darkness is not evil. Darkness is portrayed as evil because those who have no light in them fear the darkness. But those who have light in them do not fear the darkness. They are focused by it, so that they may have an impact.

This teaching from an old dwarf spirit walker was what was on the inside of the elf's mind as he moved across the lands of Xahmore` at an unrivaled speed. He had been running two days straight but felt no exhaustion in his body. His comrades were long behind him but he knew they would come. He followed a flame that burned bright and lead him through the trail of destruction left behind by the demon army and he was now but a short distance behind them.

The towns and cities on the way from the forest were all burned and massacred. Scouts were left to impede his progress but he made short work of them. He could only hear the lesson about darkness and see his mother's face. Oh the anger he had in his heart for what had been done to him, his race, and his loved ones. He clenched his teeth and ran harder when he thought of what Yorenzana planned to do. The world he was born to protect needed him now, and he remembered what his mother told him about sacrificing to be that. And he ran harder.

Suddenly atop a great hill, the flame went out and the trail went cold. He searched the entire hill for a trace and found nothing. Nothing was burned, nothing smelled of death. He ran to each side of the hill and saw nothing.

"Oh, creator," he prayed aloud, "Please show me the way. Help me to help the world. Anger has filled my heart and my mind, clear it so that I may see the way."

He fell to his knees and wept. He fell upon his face.

"You made me to be the protector, and I know now that my motivation was selfish. I am your vessel."

When he rose, he looked to where he bowed. The moonlight grazed the silver spikes in his belt, and a faint depression in the grass caught his attention. It appeared to be a human footprint. *What is a human doing out in these elfin lands alone,* he thought? Then he noticed there was blood in the grass. He pulled over his hood and set off following the prints in the grass.

He ran a couple hundred yards and in the far distance he could see a hill that appeared as its other side was on fire. It then disappeared due to the sun peaking over the far horizon.

"Thank you!" the elf said as he sprinted for the hill in the far distance.

He moved swiftly to catch the army before the sun rose and the prophecy started to take form. By the time he reached the top of the hill, the sun had already began to rise and he could see the warriors of Emolia standing on the eastern plain of the most beautiful palace made by mortal beings. There was something wrong though. As he looked from the palace, he could see a human, ragged and bloody approaching the army alone.

He must have been attacked by the demons, I thought. But where was the demon army? I will wait here in the dark. The demon army will approach soon and I will rush the plain then. The human will be helped and well out of the way by the time they come.

He watched over the plain as the human got closer and the light got closer to where he knelt on the top backside of the hill. He watched as the general from the elfin force warned the human to halt. The human did not.

I wondered why the human did not call out for help from the wounds he had sustained. Then he saw the archers shoot arrows and have the arrows returned by the human. *No*, he thought. I then saw the elves sent to attack obliterated by nothingness which had folded back to show the vast demon army that had been standing on the plain all along.

He rose to charge the plain. His foot dug into the ground to thrust him toward the demons, but he was unable to move. His entire body had become paralyzed yet suspended in his first stride. But he saw all that transpired as the battle began and continued. Elf and demon battling for the end of Xahmore' was a sight he wished to be a part of. Demons fought to free their master and elves fought to confine the beast forever.

He watched the demons' surprise appearance and quick attack put the elves at a disadvantage but he could do nothing in his present state. Tears streamed down his face.

Why is this happening? I thought to himself. *I can help stop this.*

He then saw the human walking up the wall toward the balcony. He saw what appeared to be the lead demon leading a battalion into the same path the human had walked. *Creator please let me help them!* He thought with all of his mind, heart, and soul.

The sunlight then touched the foot he had placed forward and the control of his body returned to him, he then darted off down the hill drawing his swords. His time in the darkness was done. The darkness no longer confined him. He was now the portion of the darkness that had light within it. The darkness that was him now had means to focus the light. The beginning had released its greatest warrior forged from pain. He was now a tear from the shadow.

52

THRONE OF BLOOD

The throne room, usually a place of wisdom, solace, and protected audience, was now preparing to hold audience to one of the most meaningful battles in history, the mightiest Emolia had to offer prepared to face the most evil in creation.

Smoke began to fill the orb of eyes and then it spilled over onto the floor near Blenadrene, Telaris, and the Guild of Dark Soul. The smoke then rose from the floor and began to take form into faces of anguish and pain. From inside the smoke a came a deep laugh that consumed the room. The smoke expanded and the faces became even more burdened. Then a dark figure walked forth from the smoke and the smoke became his robe outlined with a golden shoulder plates that met at his collar bone and made a long spike that pointed to the ground.

"Ahhh, my faithful servant, I see you have gathered your finest subjects to welcome me into the palace. This pleases me." said Yorenzana.

"We are not here to welcome you, foul demon. We are here to stop you or give our lives in the process of doing so." spoke Telaris as he drew a large broad sword from behind his glomasian fur cape.

"I see. Then I will be more than willing to oblige you with the latter." Yorenzana said.

Just as he said that a hundred or so of Kremlin's scavenger demons scaled the terrace and sided with Yorenzana showing their teeth and laughing in a high pitch. Yorenzana then spoke ancient words and the faces on his robe spewed white fire that covered the room. Blenadrene thwarted the fire from himself. Telaris stabbed his huge sword into the floor and ducked behind it. The guild of Dark Soul stood its ground and when the fire reached them, it revealed the armor of the elite guard that still covered them. No harm was done unto them.

"Your power makes no matter, kill them all!" Yorenzana said with disgust.

The scavengers then quickly moved in to attack the elves.

Dark Soul drew his sword and as he swung it, the blade appeared to shatter into thousands of pieces. The magical shrapnel impaled over half the scavengers going away and coming back to the base of the sword after he finished his swing. They fell to the floor dead.

Goreem then jumped over the pile of dead demons into a pack of about ten monsters. In mid-air his armor appeared and turned gold. When he landed, he was covered from head to toe with spikes and his gauntlets were blades. He began hacking the demons to bits. Every one that attacked him was impaled by a spike that extended to protect him.

Soleah and Laulare, the brother wizard and sister sorceress, who were blotted elves had telekinetic abilities whenever they touched. Each of them carried two aerial hatchets. Both tossed the weapons into the air and touched hands. Their eyes turned yellow and the hatchets circled them like wind chopping off limbs of the vile creatures as they attacked.

The rest of the demons rushed the emperor. He pulled his huge sharp broad sword that was wide enough to be his shield as well from the floor. With every swipe of his sword, demons were cut in half.

Yorenzana then spoke ancient words and the orb glowed red. Scavenger demons then began to materialize by the dozens from the sphere on the floor and kept the warriors fighting for their lives.

Probably the most important of the battles within the battles was shaping to take place. Two wizards, one ancient and the other his most decorated pupil, stared at one another intensely. The master toward over the student and the student stood firmly in front of what the master had come for.

"You are no match for me, Blenadrene, move aside or die!" spoke Yorenzana with a snarl.

"I will stand here until I am moved. If my life shall end keeping you from this door then so be it!" Blenadrene responded with conviction.

"So be it!" said Yorenzana as the robe of smoke made itself into two serpents that shot out at Blenadrene.

Blenadrene's purple robe began to glow and as the serpents reached him, he stuck his hands into both of the creatures of smoke and they split in half.

"That robe has augmented your power ten-fold. A gift from Ulrant, I suppose?" Yorenzana asked. "No matter, it will not be enough."

The demon wizard then multiplied himself so that three of him stood in front of Blenadrene. The three then reached their other two arms from under the smoke and conjured a blast that knocked Blenadrene across the throne room into a pillar busting it into pieces. The area filled with dust.

Yorenzana became one again walked towards the door of the dragons.

Blenadrene then levitated a huge piece of debris from the pillar and hurled it in the direction of Yorenzana. The huge stone caught him off guard smashing into him and sending him into a wall, pinning him.

"It will not be that easy!" proclaimed Blenadrene.

The rock was then surrounded by smoke and crumbled into dust.

"Easy enough that it will be done no matter your efforts, elf." said Yorenzana.

"Not as long as I live!" proclaimed Blenadrene.

"Fine with us," Yorenzana said as a huge red hand reached up onto the banister of the terrace.

Blenadrene had a look of terror on his face.

"You don't look so good, elf. Does something seem to have you feeling down?" asked Kremlin.

As the red demon peered over the banister at Blenadrene, his head was suddenly jerked back and there was a huge boom as he hit the ground.

Blenadrene then smiled and said, "No, demon, it is you who should feel down, my help has arrived."

"So he has, but that changes nothing, we both know that. Don't we?" Yorenzana began to laugh and walked towards the door of the dragons.

53

THE KEY

As I reached the battlefield, he paid no mind to the lesser demons that tried to attack him. He just moved through the fight dodging everything thrown at him. His eyes were fixated on the big red demon that he had been tracking for two days which had began to scale the wall to enter the same place the human had gone. The demon's hand reached the banister of the balcony and as he peered over the banister into the throne room into Blenadrene's eyes. I leaped from close to a hundred yards out and landed on the back of Kremlin's neck choking him with his assassin's bands. The demon fell back, I pulled hard and jumped, the demon flipped over onto the ground face first. BOOM!!

As the dust settled, I threw one of his silver spikes high into the air. Kremlin rose from the depression his fall created in the ground with a look to murder whoever was the cause of his fall. The pain from the fall caused Kremlins's four horns to shift from upward to back.

"Hello, Kremlin. Are you prepared to die?" asked I.

"Ahh you have finally caught up with me. How many bodies did you have to leap to reach me?" asked the demon.

"All the ones you left standing in my way. Now there is only one body I have to leap on my way to my destination." I said as he charged Kremlin.

I then leaped into the air. Kremlin looked up to keep I in his sight and the spike I hurled up a short time before pierced the demon warlord's left eye.

"Agghh!" screamed the red demon as he dropped his spiked club, and his chest went from a pectoral look to a barreled shape.

I then came down from high above with his swords drawn and stabbed into the demon's back on each side of his spine and slid down his massive back catching the demon's back on fire. This caused the demon to raise up and come down on all fours transforming into a bullish type monster.

Kremlin began to kick and buck to try and remove the elf from his back. I removed his swords from Kremlins's back and flipped off him and landed in front of Kremlin, then sheathed his swords.

"Demon, your days have come to an end. You will now pay your debt to those you have slain in cold blood." said I

Kremlin said nothing, his bloodstained, bullish face just showed a smile. He saw his death lizard sneaking up on I and just waited until it moved to strike the blotted elf down. The lizard stayed low and crept softly. When it was within striking range, it lunged itself at I with its mouth wide open showing jagged teeth and saliva. Just as it was about to clamp its jaws onto I, a loud roar came from nowhere and Muline tackled the huge lizard to the ground. Muline then lifted his huge paw-like fist and bashed the lizard's head in. The army of light had arrived.

I turned his attention back to the injured demon warlord in front of him. Kremlin charged I and lowered his head showing I the tips of his four horns. I pulled his staff and leapt into the sky to gather the strength needed.

As he came down, he brought the staff above his head and stuck down upon Kremlins's head, smashing his skull. The beast's warlord crashed to the ground and slid across the battlefield. I then looked hard at Kremlin until he saw a dark spot close to his heart. I walked up to the demon who was even larger in his true form.

"As you have shown no love, you shall leave here with no heart." said the black-eyed blotted elf.

I then reached into the dark area and snatched the black heart out of the warlord of the beast, the demon released his last breath and died.

The army of light rushed the valley with such power that the demon army stood no chance.

Muline, Rimleon, and Mlar joined their friend under the terrace.

"What now?" asked Mlar.

I said nothing, he just lept to the terrace and his friends followed. He walked into the throne room and observed the battle taking place. Yorenzana had Blenadrene in his hands about to cast a spell. He watched as elves fought with purpose to stay alive in a pool of demons. He saw how the scavenger demons were materializing from the sphere on the floor, so he walked over to it. He picked it up.

"That may have been a mistake, young hero." said Yorenzana as he tried to take control of the black-eyed elf's mind.

"I can feel you trying, demon, but the mistake seems to be yours." I replied.

The eyes that resembled Yorenzana's in the sphere faded away. The sphere then turned pitch-black.

"Just how strong are you, child?" asked the demon wizard with a hint of confusion.

"Let us find out." I said.

"Let us not." Yorenzana replied as he reached into the smoke of his robe and removed Dinora who lay limp in his hand.

"Mother!" I cried out as he reached toward her.

"Yes, boy, now we shall end this!" Yorenzana said in the most evil of tones.

I gripped the sphere tightly and thought how he wished he could destroy all the demons in the room and the sphere released a black wave of energy. The wave destroyed all the scavenger demons on contact and knocked Yorenzana from his feet causing him to release Blenadrene and Dinora.

There was only one thing that clouded this moment. Dinora's unconscious body had landed on the door of the dragons. Yorenzana chuckled softly and dissipated into smoke.

54

First of the Fallen

There are some things that are destined to happen, no matter how hard we try and stop them. No matter how much we plan and execute, some things are just meant to be. The thing is, after those things show that they cannot be cut out of destiny, how do you react?

I rushed to his mother's side.

"Mother, mother." said I intently as the rest of the elves looked on.

She said nothing. She did not even move. Her body lay in I's arms hot and barely breathing. Mlar flew in onto his friend's shoulder.

"Is she okay?" Mlar asked.

"I don't know." I said with tears in his eyes.

Her body then jerked, and her eyes opened with a purple hue, the hue of Ulrant.

"Get her away from the door!" yelled Blenadrene.

I lifted her and began to walk from the middle of the door. The hue in her eyes left and her eyes turned back to her natural grey color. But the floor beneath them now held the hue. The crystal shard had fallen from Dinora's head onto the door. Blenadrene rushed to try and pick it up, but as he reached for it, a white hand of mist came through the cracks of the door and pulled the shard into the stone.

"No. We have failed, just as Ulrant told me we would."
Blenadrene said softly.

He rushed to the terrace to warn the warriors out side.

"Run. leave here and do not look back!"

The very ground began to shake.

Dinora spoke to I for the first time in what seemed
like forever.

"Son, what is happening?"

"We have failed to stop the demons. The door is
beginning to open. The beast will be free. All is lost." he said.

"No, my son, this is but one day. This one day may be lost
but the war will rage on."

Mahalia walked over to give Dinora her cloak. The elves
in the throne room all gathered on the west side of the door
and watched as the huge stones that it was made of open
into the ceiling causing it to break apart and part of it to fall
into the deep hole that was lit by a sea of fire. The rumbling
stopped. There was a deafening silence.

Suddenly there were thousands upon thousands of
winged demons shooting up out of the open hole through
the ceiling and spreading all over Xahmore. The flow of
demons did not stop. Then there was a shadow in the midst
of the winged demons. It was shaped like a man but when
it opened its eyes they where a glowing white.

A booming voice then spoke so loud, the entire world
could hear.

"My minions, I am free and Xahmore is once again
under my rule. You may now come from your hiding places
and do as you see fit to the world."

At his command, the most evil of beings began to
conspire and run wild upon Xahmore'.

"I must stop him!" said I as he walked from the grouping of elves toward the door drawing his swords.

"Not yet my son" Dinora said as she looked at her son with the same blue glow in her eyes that she had on the lower deck of the Glynasha.

"No, Dinora!" said Blenadrene, "that spell will destroy you!"

"But it will spare you all, so that all will not be lost." she shouted to her mentor.

Just then the shadowy figure noticed the gathering and spotted the blotted black-eyed elf.

"You!!" the beast said as he stretched forth a hand and released a blast that cooked the air on the way to the area where the gathering was.

Dinora stood in front of them all and as the blast reached her it turned into a beautiful shimmering light as if the moon graced a diamond. Then there was silence.

When the light subsided; I, Blenadrene, Mlar, Rimleon, Muline, Telaris, and the Guild of Dark Soul were in a diamond-like dome and standing at the front of it with her body now a solid diamond statue was Dinora. Once I realized what had taken place, he screamed out in agony and began to weep uncontrollably.

"Why mother, why? I could have protected you all." He screamed.

"What did she do?" asked Rimleon.

"She cast a spell created by Leana called All My Love." answered Blenadrene in an emotional tone. "Her love for her son allowed her to conjure a spell that protected us all from the brunt of the beast."

The beast attacked the diamond dome again and again. It became infuriated! Nothing it did could get through the casing that held the warriors. It screamed and growled. It changed forms hundreds of times trying to get into the stone to the blotted elf but could not. It then knocked down the palace, so that the inhabitants of the dome could see what it was about to do. It took the form of a two-headed dragon and flew into the clouds and above. He spoke words that fell red into the clouds.

It then began to rain stones of fire upon all the land. The beast then came down and landed in front of the dome with force that shook the ground. He walked up to it in the form of a grey monster with six eyes on its face. It reached its face close to the diamond-like stone, creating thousands of threatening reflections. And he spoke.

"I will be waiting for you, boy, for now I must find the ones who had me imprisoned for so long and repay them for their defiance, but our time will come!" the beast said with malice.

"I long for it." I replied just as harsh.

"Until then, child!" The beast said as he imploded to a dot and vanished.

The Withering was now upon Xahmore`.

"What happened after that Wise elder?" asked Lorimeck with bright eyes. "Who did the beast hunt? How did they get out of the diamond? Was his mother dead?"

Then little Feloshia chimed in, "What happened to Yorenzana? Did I ever destroy the beast?"

"Hmmm, another story for another time young ones, the great rain is approaching quickly from the south. You should go and get ready for the feast."

"Okay we will, but promise us you will tell us the rest of the story." said Lorimeck.

"I promise, little ones."

"Come on, Feloshia. We will be back, wise elder. Once the feast is in order and we have eaten. Would you like us to bring you anything?"

"No, I have all I need."

My young, I hope they return as soon as they can. This story is one I have never told, and it brings back such adventurous memories. The Withering was very harsh and at times seemed like it would never end.

But you too will have to wait on the young ones to return to hear of it as well old friend.

Yes, there are parts about the black-eyed blotted elf that even you do not know. But I will tell you that the Beast was not the only one to return to the world by way of the Dragon's door that day.

Who was it, you might ask? Let's just say our hero would have been better off if they would have remained where they were.

.